ALSO BY JOSEPH COLWELL

FROM LICHEN ROCK PRESS

NATURE ESSAY COLLECTIONS

Canyon Breezes: Exploring Magical Places in Nature

Zephyr of Time: Meditations on Time and Nature

Echoes of Time: Reflections on the Mesas and Canyons of the Dominguez-Escalante National Conservation Area

FICTION

Tales of Ravens Nest: A Life, A Place: Stories and Reflections
(Book Two of the *Ravens Nest* trilogy)

The Hermit of Puccini Ridge
(Book One of the *Ravens Nest* trilogy)

MEMOIR

Tuscola: A Memoir
Place, Time, and Meanings of a Hometown

FROM PAGE PUBLISHING

FICTION

Sands of Time: A Flight of Discovery and Search for Meanings of Time

Flight of the RAVEN

ENDING *and* BEGINNING

JOSEPH COLWELL

Lichen Rock Press
Hotchkiss, Colorado 81419

An early version of the essay "Winter Solstice" was included in Colwell's 2018 *Echoes of Time* under the title "Eagle Rock: Winter Solstice", pages 117-122.

Editing
Katherine Colwell

Photography
Katherine Colwell
Joseph Colwell

Design and Publishing Services
Connie King
Constance King Design

Lichen Rock Press
Hotchkiss, Colorado
ColwellCedars.com

ISBN: 978-0-9962222-6-6
Printed in USA

Author's Note

This collection of essays and short stories completes a literary journey begun innocently enough nearly two decades ago, and blossomed as new stories surfaced. As with my previous volumes based on the memoirs of the fictional Jake Collins and a place called Ravens Nest—"Tales of Ravens Nest" (2018) and "Hermit of Puccini Ridge" (2022)—I rely on my personal experiences, knowledge, truth, and imagination.

The novella *Opal's Story*, Part One of "The Hermit of Puccini Ridge," was secretly written by the recently retired Jake, and was the second manuscript edited and published by the fictional Alistaire Corey after he and his wife discovered a second stash of Jake's writings. The tantalizing historical information about the old recluse who homesteaded and occupied the property before it became Ravens Nest, was gathered through interviews and research by this author.

"Tales of Ravens Nest" is comprised of Jake's novella *Tori's Dream*, essays and short stories (including Jake and Rachel's last years at Ravens Nest), and a selection of Jake's career experiences in government agencies throughout the West. Bernice Sanderson, Tori Reynold's assistant, edited the updated second edition of "Tales," to include Tori's final years after Alistaire passed.

In "Flight of the Raven," circumstances happened long after "Hermit" and "Tales" were published; Jake was long gone. The destruction of the main house at Ravens Nest resulted in long-time caretaker Bernice Sanderson finding more of Jake's writings. But those long-hidden stories and—as Jake calls them—ramblings, inspired me to gather them into what becomes here the third volume of the Ravens Nest trilogy.

Organized in six parts, the essays range in subject matter from Jake's career (more truth than fiction), further tales about the place called Ravens Nest, and much of the older Jake's philosophy. My guess is Jake was putting on paper his thoughts and philosophy, knowing his final days might catch up to him unaware. Ravens played an important role, so it is fitting that the end of Jake's journey concerns the ravens taking flight and leaving.

~ Joseph Colwell

Contents

PART IV: TORI'S SONGS

PART V: REFLECTIONS ON A SENSE OF PLACE

PART VI: LOST IN TIME

PART VII: BERNICE SANDERSON'S EPILOGUE

Preface
Editor Bernice Sanderson

It has been many years since I added the final chapters to the revised edition of "Tales of Ravens Nest," and I have been living and working at Ravens Nest these past decades. Now it is time for me to depart. I love the place and all the people who manage it, but as kind as everyone is to me, I know now that I am an anachronism. I have seen Ravens Nest in its mid-life years and have watched many changes; my old world has disappeared.

I did not know the original owners, but I heard many stories from both Tori and Al about Jake's and Rachel's love of the land. Al edited the first edition of "Tales of Ravens Nest," a collection of stories and essays found among Jake's files, with instructions for Al on publishing.

Not long after I came to Ravens Nest, Al succumbed to pancreatic cancer, and I became a confidante and assistant to Tori—an internationally acclaimed singer, song writer, musician—for her remaining years. She considered Jake a mentor and father figure, and shared with me another collection of Jake's writing that he had secretly given to her. These essays were written for her, and he'd asked her to not tell Al or anyone else about them. Over the years, Tori was inspired by, and incorporated parts of, these writings into her lyrics. However, Tori did not know about Jake's final essays, written a few days before his passing, nor did she know the extent of what Jake had written—the essays and stories in this volume.

When Tori passed, we were in the process of turning over management and ownership to the Ute Tribal Council, in the form of Ravens Nest Institute. This was all consistent with Jake's and Rachel's wishes. As I read more of Jake's writing, I understand his feelings in old age, and see the same happening to me now. My widowed niece, Laura, has asked me to live with her; shortly before my long-time partner Robbie passed away, I visited Laura at her small sheep ranch on South Island, New Zealand.

Robin Wind Feather came to work at Ravens Nest shortly after I did. Robbie was Nuche (or Ute), with a very interesting heritage. Her ancestors also included Chinese (from pioneer days 150 years ago), Black (from a buffalo soldier about that same time), and Anglo (from the pioneers who took over the land the Nuche lived on for over 10,000 years). Robbie was part of this land and the people who helped settle it and is now buried on this, her ancestral land.

Robbie had a special gift—not only in tending the gardens and animals of Ravens Nest—but also 'powers' I would call shamanic. She could feel ancestral energy and on more than one occasion stood on a piece of land and said her ancestors were buried there. Maybe a small pile of rocks or a slight rise in the ground told me she was probably correct. She talked with the ravens, hawks, and eagles, and sometimes one flying over would swoop low over her head, then rise high in the sky. To be honest, it freaked me out, but she was the most thoughtful and courteous person I've ever met. I miss you Robbie and you are with your ancestors again. May you fly with the ravens and eagles.

After Tori passed, I stayed on as a caretaker to guide and advise the Council as specified in the Trust agreement worked out between Tori and the Council. I did not expect this but was honored to help due to the depth of my familiarity with Ravens Nest; Robbie helped me immensely with this.

Several months after Robbie passed, the first earthquake hit western Colorado. It shook the Ravens Nest buildings, but didn't cause any damage. I was working in the greenhouse the chilly April morning when that first quake hit and I remember well the ground shaking and the swaying baskets full of blooming geraniums and pansies. Geologists' consensus was that type of activity and that type of earth structure did not exist here, but within a month, there were two more quakes. Millions of years ago this area was quite active: the San Juan and West Elk mountain ranges were centers of volcanic activity; and Grand Mesa, just a few miles north, was covered with basalt flows. All that activity and the reasons for it did not exist anymore; at least that was the scientific opinion. But things changed quickly; the first earthquake woke people up, although most people thought it was due to the abundance of natural gas drilling and fracking occurring in the general area. Whether it was or not will probably never be proven. But whatever the cause, something significant changed miles below the surface.

Smaller quakes continued to shake the area until the 'big one' hit several months later, registering over seven on the Richter scale. It devasted not only this immediate area but much of western Colorado. In several areas nearby, hot springs surfaced; and geologists warned the public something significant was happening: lava began seeping out faults that had opened.

The big one did unrepairable damage to the original Ravens Nest house, and other buildings were damaged but repairable. We all decided to raze the house, and in the process, we discovered a safe in the crawl space. It was mostly buried, but the top was exposed; a scrap of carpet had lain over the safe and no one knew it was there. It was obviously not placed there for theft protection since the combination to the lock was written on the safe door. The Council members and I guessed it was for fire protection. Within the safe was a collection of papers and old computer drives, the contents of which make up the majority of the work in this volume. The technology was old, but with help I was able to retrieve it.

Of course, these were hidden and not available when Al put together the first edition, and I, the second edition, of "Tales of Ravens Nest." They are in the same vein, although a significant portion are Jake's autobiographical essays recounting some of the more political 'adventures' of his career (Parts One and Two). In addition, a collection of short nature essays reflect on Ravens Nest itself (Part Three); and Jake's philosophy is woven throughout. I thought of putting these essays together with a selection of photographs taken over the years by Rachel and Tori, but decided to assemble the earthquake-trove as this third and final volume the Ravens Nest trilogy.

Jake and Rachel called their property Ravens Nest for good reason. Ravens—Corvus corax—love this location, yearly building nests and raising their young. Flocks of ravens seasonally fly over, calling and cawing. A pair or more of ravens sit on power poles or trees near the buildings, and tease the dogs. Jake and Rachel taught Al and Tori to talk with the birds, and Tori taught me, but Robbie surpassed all our efforts in communicating with these profoundly intelligent birds. She would invite them to land next to her, occasionally even able to touch them. As I leave, my connection with the ravens ends. They may take flight in my mind, but I am sure they will continue to live and enchant this property.

In this collection, Jake explains why he hid the writings that make up Parts One and Two. (Most of his earlier stories about his career adventures were just that—his adventures). In his 'Utah stories', he describes experiences, along with discussions about them and the people he dealt with. He was afraid he came across as rough on the communities and people, expressing his frustrations and some negative feelings about those he lived and worked with. Based on my knowledge of Jake, he had a decent reputation, and even though he had no plans to publish any of his work, he was afraid to diminish his reputation by telling some of these stories. I think he knew they would come out eventually, so hid them until a date far enough in the future that no one would be left alive who would recognize any of the people. I think he achieved that. With that understanding, I feel comfortable including these in this volume. I think Jake was ahead of his time in trying to show his respect and reverence for the land. As he has said, that was his job.

Part Four encompasses the essays that Jake secretly shared with Tori, which she was inspired by, and used a few words or phrases in her lyrics. His essays helped form much of her thinking.

Parts Five and Six reflect Jake's deeper philosophical beliefs. The *sense of place* essays reflect his love of the concept and he wrote many variations. He spent his lifetime seeking others' wisdom and learning from his own life, through asking questions that have been asked by learned sages for centuries. I think he knew most of these questions have no answers, but wanted to capture the essence of his life and the meaning of his life. Jake loved the long geologic history of this scenic area of the West. I expect he would be pleased to see it continue in surprising and powerful ways.

THE HIDDEN LEGACY

This collection rambles—just as my life rambled until setting down roots in this special place. Alistaire and Tori will ensure that Ravens Nest itself is a legacy from all four of us, but I have more to add.

Throughout many decades, I've documented my thoughts as a written historical legacy. Rachel has always encouraged me to include a memoir of my career; I wrote a lot about it, but never a comprehensive manuscript. Bits and pieces abound, and there are more bits and pieces among these ramblings. I am leaving instructions for Al about publishing two collections: "Tales of Ravens Nest" and "Hermit of Puccini Ridge."

As the sunset of my life approaches, I am leaving some of these writings within easy sight, and leaving some of these hidden, to be discovered (if ever) long into the future. This may confuse and confound people, but at that point I certainly won't care. Several of the final essays may indicate otherwise; I wanted to keep some of these hidden since I most likely offend some of the people I write about.

Pondering, quantifying and pinning down the essence of Ravens Nest as a special place led to my series of short essays *The Senses of a Place*. We all need a sense of place and we will all be better off if we find at least one, somewhere or sometime in our lives.

I may be around in some form, but not the one I am currently in. I will let the reader decide if there is any chance of that.

~Jake Collins

Part I

A Western Bureaucrat

Bernice Sanderson's Introduction

After Jake's passing, among the manuscripts that Alistaire Corey found were short stories about Jake's career working within federal and state agencies throughout the west. Though fictionalized and often using different names and other minor details, Alistaire felt they were true because Jake had often talked about them. As Jake aged, he repeated many of his adventures so often, Alistaire could almost tell them himself. "Tales of Ravens Nest" (2018) included nine of these stories.

In this volume, Part One is comprised of four more, ranging from early to late in his career; and the five stories in Part Two are devoted to Jake's 'Utah Years'.

The Three-Decades Wild Ride

Springtime in the Black Hills of South Dakota, 1997. Grass was greening up and deciduous trees leafing out. Riding Buck down an old, closed logging road, I sat back in the saddle. My mind wandered to similar experiences of the past three decades.

May was a time I always anticipated—time to get out into the field after a long winter behind a desk. The world was waking up; snow was melting and I was arranging my priorities for the upcoming summer. No seasonal employees were working for me yet and I had time to myself. Soon, though, after a short summer, I would wish for winter again so I could relax from the onslaught of summer projects, supervision head-aches, budget worries, un-met targets, and assorted other reasons to long for cold snowy months. Seems the season for enjoying this job was short indeed.

Riding just for the fun of it. On a horse this mild spring day in my 50th year of life; I could cover ground just as well and twice as fast on a 4-wheeler or in a pickup. The Black Hills doesn't have the backcountry like on the Dixie National Forest in Utah or the North Park District of the Routt National Forest in northern Colorado. I missed that. But you make do with what you have. So I loaded Buck and drove to the Higgins Gulch Cattle Allotment to look for projects for the National Guard to do during their massive encampment in the upcoming weeks. Memories flooded my mind. I had exciting and excruciating interactions with the military in other locations—building duck ponds, blasting rock cliffs, and building roads (fig.3). More often, I'd sweated over them: getting their D-9 dozers stuck in the middle of a wet meadow, blowing up a ton of excess dynamite, or frittering away precious moments drinking coffee, while wondering why I used the Army Reserve or National Guard to accomplish project targets. Well—once more with feeling, I thought. One last time to work with the boys in camouflage.

Rounding a bend in the road, I identified a location for a small water pond, and stopped to talk into my tape recorder. Buck perked his ears. Ahead of us six elk wandered off the slope of a hill and crossed the road. I sat and watched in subdued awe. Buck talked with his ears. We both were fascinated as ten, twenty, forty cows and calves crossed.

They bleated and cried as I tried to answer their strange sounds. Buck's backward flip of his ears indicated his displeasure with my poor imitation. This reminded me of times in Colorado when I watched dozens of elk or deer cross through meadows and forest. Moose, deer, antelope, spotted owls—wildlife is in my blood. My college degree was in wildlife management, but I rarely had opportunities to practice intensive wildlife management. As with many other things, I managed to give a lick and a promise to habitat improvement projects. But I was spread too thin, with too much to do and usually very little money in the wildlife budget. I thought: not for much longer.

A heavy load was melting from my shoulders. I was taking early retirement in two months and this was my swan song. It was strange how things were suddenly falling into place and priorities seemed to sort themselves out quite nicely. They say a short-timer has the best attitude. I agree. I just didn't care about a lot of things anymore. The meetings, the budgetary nonsense, the ridiculous regulations, and policy. No more worries about how this or that decision might affect my career.

My career was down the tubes and basically had been from the first day I walked into the LaJara office my very first day of work in 1970 wearing a ridiculous Hawaiian shirt. I was fresh from marriage on the rim of the Grand Canyon and a one-day honeymoon spent driving across the Navajo Reservation. All the rest of my clothes were packed in the car my brother-in-law was driving and he was nowhere to be seen. I started with the Forest Service in the wrong place with the wrong boss. Although I had many good adventures, I never was in the right place at the right time. Well, their loss. But for right now, that was behind me, many waters under many bridges.

As I watched the last elk cross into the birch thicket, I thought back on this career with the Forest Service, USDA. Inspired by Lassie and Corey Stuart, both now long in their graves, I left my home and youth in Illinois and went West. Strange how one turn led to another. Roads not taken and paths diverted. Lots of ifs, and even though I knew not to think about them, they still haunted me occasionally. I started work on the Rio Grande National Forest, Conejos Ranger District (fig. 1) in late June of 1970. Times were certainly different then. I was as green as my uniform and didn't have a clue about what my job entailed. But I was in Colorado, I had a permanent job, I lived in a cabin by a river in the mountains, got to ride a horse, and worked in my very own wilderness of trees and streams and elk (fig. 2). I could learn all the rest as I went.

Well—I went, and I learned. And my journey went from the Rio Grande and the land of DeAnza to the wildlife haven of North Park and the North Platte River. Then one of those quirky turns of fate and I found myself in East Lansing, Michigan, in a huge university with more people than all the counties I had lived in the past ten years combined. I was studying resource economics, planning, and policy analysis so I could continue on a slightly different career path. There, I struggled to become something I wasn't cut out to be. Freshly retrained, I followed the route of wagons-west 130 years earlier. I looked for my gold in California, on the Tahoe National Forest—land of tall trees, poison oak, and the "handcuffs" of an office and theoretical planning. I say theoretical because I lost touch with reality with the land. The planning took four years of my life but continued on without me with a life of its own. I think after 10 years, they finally got a Plan, but I lost interest much before then. Chalk up one big one for world-class skepticism and disillusionment. Also, chalk up one for a career lost in the shuffle and my struggle to get back to where I belonged. I never quite made it.

But along the way, I met spotted owls and encountered over-harvested watersheds. I fought with ranchers and their 19th century pioneer mentality. I struggled with the internal politics of bureaucratic power, and lost big time. I explored aspen groves and alpine tundra in Colorado, and the slickrock canyons of southern Utah. I fell in love with the land everywhere, but became dis-illusioned with people. Too bad, but stereotypes do count for something. I then drifted to the birch and aspen and pine forests of the Black Hills, sacred to Lakota and many others.

So that's where I sat, on good ol' Buck, looking for projects for the National Guard. Twenty-seven years into a career that many people would trade for in a minute. Unfortunately, I was still looking for what I wanted to do, unable to find it in the millennium-ending confusion and disintegration that was the Forest Service of 1997. The decades had seen the agency go from 'white-hat' to 'black-hat'. From respected to universally scorned. From my innocent wanderings, searching for my place in a fledgling career, to a cynical end in early retirement.

But I needed time to reflect on just what my career meant. A ride on Buck along a deserted forest road, watching bluebirds soar overhead, listening to elk cry to each other as they left one drainage and headed over the hill—I realized this was what it was all about. This feeling, this freedom, this experience was why I chose this career. I only had a few weeks left. I would enjoy it while I could and think more about the good times I had. People would indeed trade places with me. I needed to simply focus on the good times. Buck would take care of me while my mind wandered.

Horses were an interesting part of some of my adventures. My first time on horseback—officially that is—I was helping move cattle on the Cumbres Cattle Allotment on the Conejos District. I had no idea what I was doing, but as I rode along, looking every part the tenderfoot misplaced in some sappy Western, I felt proud. I'm lucky I didn't fall off the horse. But it got in my blood. I soon bought my own horse but had no saddle or trailer. My boss didn't like the idea, but I didn't care. I owned a horse. Within a year, I sold her. I called her Brandy, short for Brandywine, the river bordering the shire in Tolkien's "Lord of the Rings." I was like a furry hobbit in my own ring quest, not sure where I was going, but bouncing along, one adventure after another. I spent one summer day looking for a horse that bounded off when I dismounted to eat lunch. He belonged to the local game warden and it turned out I unknowingly used him without permission. Seems like I often spent more time trying to catch horses in the expansive horse pastures than I did riding them. But I never got kicked; I never killed a horse or lost one. I even learned how to tie a diamond hitch on a packhorse—which spelled success in this outfit.

I was trying to do something good for the permittees on the Higgins Allotment, although within a few weeks, I found them turning on me big time. They weren't my favorites, but I'd had much worse. Grazing permittees were like many people; I'd met and worked with very good ones whom I admired, and I'd met and worked with some real horses' asses. They probably helped do me in and break my spirit as much as anything. The East Slope Allotment on the Teasdale District in Utah was my Waterloo. I spent two years working on a case to reduce cattle numbers on a grossly overstocked range. I fought ranchers who lived in the last century in a wild land that they—like their grandfathers—were sent to tame. I fought that to a standstill and I don't think it has been settled to this day almost a decade later. I fought ranchers right here on this Higgins Allotment who couldn't grasp the concept that they were only one part of the use of this land. People would much rather see an elk than a domestic moo-cow. But could these ranchers understand that? My task on the Higgins Allotment was to develop more water for them so the cows could better use all this allotment (fig. 4). And the Army would help me do that. It was a parting shot of kindness on my part, but it was soon met with a parting shot by the permittees.

After the elk disappeared into the birch forest, Buck and I continued down the road into a dandelion-filled meadow. Yellow with the bloom of this invasive weed, it should be grass green, and dotted with a profusion of native wildflowers. This to me was indicative of the battles I had fought. Decades of overgrazing had destroyed much of the native flora. Most people wouldn't notice. I did, and like many crusaders, I paid the price of zeal. My battles would soon be over and I would leave the crusade to others. Like the battle-scarred veteran, I was to walk away from the front line, my dignity bruised but intact. I thought about what I had achieved. Twenty-seven years is a long time and much had changed in my beloved West. But in my profession, three decades is nothing. It is not time for an overgrazed dandelion meadow to return to marsh muhly grass, green needlegrass, phlox, and asters. It is not time for a gully deepened by overgrazing-induced runoff to silt in and grow sedges and cutthroat. It is not time for a fire-charred sagebrush flat to come back in bitterbrush and muley fawns. It is not time for the clear-cut spruce hillsides of Wolf Creek Pass to wave fluttering green in aspen sprouts and butterflies. It is enough time to have tried and started a process of change. People do change and the land does endure. Abused lands will recover and people will learn respect. I hope.

Buck led me where he wanted. I was lost in time. We crossed meadows, followed old logging tracks, crossed from pine to birch forests, down hollows, and up slopes to hilltops. Much too soon, I returned to the present and headed Buck towards the main road. He and his companions branded with US on the right flank, had carried me and my colleagues branded with a tree symbol and a badge on our left pocket flap. We had shared a quest and now it was time for me to leave them all and ride into my sunset.

Those past three decades had been a wild ride and I needed to reflect on the good things. Geese circling in uniform confusion on a windy April morning. Moose trucked in from Utah charging down the trail upon release from their holding pen into the North Park, Colorado, willow bottoms. Peregrine falcon chicks being carried in a wide mouth thermos up to the prairie falcon nest on a California cliff. The unbelievable expanse of tundra above the Conejos River canyon as an August thunderstorm unleashed its lightning fury on me, my wife, my dog, and the horses. The feeling of over-seeing completion of the Rim Trail along the edge of Boulder Top—with a view of an expanse of Utah slickrock wilderness larger than half of the original 13 states. Stepping outside the National Interagency Fire Center in Boise in 100-degree heat, needing a break from spending 20 days on the telephone to reporters from around the world during the fires of '94, and watching the Chicken Complex fifty miles away explode in a towering billow of smoke. Sitting by a burning log at 2:00 a.m. with Paddy and Joe after hiking five miles in the dark to find and fight a fire near the LaGarita Wilderness. Watching the California National Guard blow up nearly a ton of dynamite they didn't have time to use for blasting potholes, ducking behind my pickup as dirt and rock flew by from half a mile away, and being deafened by a Vietnam-sized explosion. Listening to a spotted owl hoot, an elk bugle, coyotes howl, antelope snort, falcons chirp, and crickets sing near a campfire in the wilderness. Watching the sunrise light up Mt. Zirkel after a light October dusting of snow covered our tent miles from the nearest road.

Yes—it was all worth it. Satisfaction often comes with frustration, but regardless of rewards or lack of them, it does come. And I will always think of the good things I did for the land and its future inhabitants. As I spend my retirement on forty acres of my very own forest, I will watch the sandhill cranes head north in the spring and return home in the fall. The mule deer and bobcats will walk my trails and forage on my newly planted trees. Just up the road, the aspen leaves will swirl and whirl to the ground just before the heavy snows of Colorado melt them into nourishment for the avalanche lily in the spring. It has always happened and it always will. Others will continue the effort to do the right thing and keep the wildlands for the next generation of expectant high school seniors who pack for a new life in new lands.

Buck snorted in agreement as I told myself out loud I did a good job after all, helping guide proper use of the land for a few short years. I kicked Buck into a gallop as we headed back to the truck. The wind blew in my face as we sped through the hills. A mountain bluebird followed us for a while, then soared off out of sight.

North Park: Moose

New to my assignment in northern Colorado in 1976, I did a quick study on the history and wildlife of this high mountain valley. With what I found and what I could see, I immediately called this a wildlife paradise. It and the surrounding mountains of wilderness peaks, valleys, streams, and meadows, abounded in nearly all the original wildlife, with four exceptions. Grizzlies, wolves, bison, and moose had disappeared in the past 100 years. Almost. Wolves were occasionally claimed to be seen and moose did wander down from Wyoming. However, the moose were always shot by a myopic hunter, thinking it was an elk. Wolves faded into the mists but always suggested a silent return. Bison, in semi-domesticated form occasionally showed up courtesy of an innovative rancher. Griz was probably gone forever.

As I explored my new territory, I was intrigued by the river bottoms. Rivers and streams flowed from all directions into the high-elevation valley called North Park. Many of the streams were so clogged by willow thickets, it was hard to find the water. When one did claw through the jungles of ten-foot-tall willows, the beaver dams created ponds and wetlands that defied easy passage. "This is moose heaven," I thought. My impression was justified when during my first month in North Park, I read in the paper of a moose being shot just south of the Wyoming border. How often had these creatures wandered down from Wyoming or Utah, been immediately mistaken for a deer or an elk, and shot?

It was also the thought of officials in the Colorado Division of Wildlife (DOW) and had been for years. Finally, someone decided it was time to act. The growing environmental movement was catching the attention of many people. During my first summer there, I was charged with the research and creation of an Environmental Assessment (EA)—a lesser sibling of the more bureaucratic clogged Environmental Impact Statement (EIS)—for the introduction of moose. This was technically a proposal by the Colorado DOW, because the state owns the wildlife, while the U. S. Forest Service owns the land. This seemed to be such an easy assignment, I naively thought. Moose are rather easy-going creatures, as graceful as ballerinas dancing in a summer breeze, though clearly the ugliest thing around. Who could be against moose?

A lot of local ranchers, I discovered. Of course, many local ranchers were against anything proposed by a governmental agency—state or federal. But that came later. First, I had to determine if the habitat would support moose. They love willow bottoms; just look at any painting of moose standing in a lake, muzzle dripping with water and pond weeds. I discovered that even though willows are utilized by moose, they were not necessary. I was fond of saying that moose did not read textbooks; they eat a variety of plants, not all dependent on lakes and streams. They do not eat grass, thus they would not crowd out bossy and toro, the lovable bovines that local ranchers pay to graze and often overgraze river bottoms. They can easily hop a six-foot-high fence. And moose are notoriously solitary so there is no need to worry about a herd of moose destroying everything in their path.

Gathering my meager supply of summer helpers and the occasional bureaucrat who wondered what I was doing, I collected a tape measure, a willow identification book, and chest waders, and hit the willow bottoms of the Michigan River. More accurately, they hit me like a sledgehammer. I had intended to walk transects through the willows and count the willow stems, seeing if they were listed as the type preferred by moose. My plea that moose didn't read textbooks fell on deaf ears. Data was needed and it needed to be accurate.

It took me an entire afternoon to convince my boss it was impossible to walk, wade, or even cut a way through the typical willow thickets. After taking him out to a willow patch and struggling to walk ten feet in anything resembling a straight line, he understood my dilemma. Short of a helicopter or hot air balloon—neither of which was in my budget—we couldn't do it. We couldn't even find the river, which we knew by aerial photo was somewhere out there. The one time I did manage to wend my way through—certainly not by any Euclidean idea of a straight line—I found myself at the edge of a series of beaver dams and ponds that made me wonder if I had somehow wandered off course to the wilderness of northern Minnesota and the Boundary Waters canoe country.

The Forest Wildlife Biologist came over from the Supervisor's office in Steamboat Springs to give me a hand. I forever after wish I'd had a video camera to document this assistance. I and my one-man crew that day were standing by our vehicle at the road intersection where we were to meet Jim. He arrived as scheduled and slowly got out of his truck. Being a good old boy, he stood up to his full six-foot height as he unwound from his truck seat, spit a wad of chew, looked at me, and looked at the wall of willows beyond the hundred-foot expanse of wide-open meadow. He looked again at the willow thicket, and drawled, "Good God A'mighty and Jesus, too. What the hell are we supposed to do? Walk into that? This is a joke, right?" He pushed his glasses up on his nose, took out his can of tobacco, stuffed a wad behind his lip, and adjusted his hat.

"No, Jim, you were called over here to help me inventory this. We have to run a few one-hundred-yard transects and measure the height, spread, and species every ten feet. Want to measure or record?" I smiled. Jim didn't. He spit again, took off his Stetson and wiped his forehead, then said, "Well, let's do it."

Picking the location for the transect on the aerial photo was the easy part. We were standing right where we would start. Identifying one willow leaf from another needed DNA analysis. I prided myself on plant identification, but this was more impossible than counting willow plants. There are more species of willows than there are of mosquitos. And they all look the same. Both willow and mosquito.

Jim never forgave me, but did help to back me up in proving there was no way to get any scientific data that was worth anything. Everyone knew this area would support moose, lots of moose, and for the purpose of this study, that was enough.

I did come up with some data, which I obfuscated to the point of head-shaking indifference. Bureaucratic report writing did have some advantages. My summary was something along the line of "food is abundant for a large population of moose." My unwritten challenge was for anyone to prove otherwise. The Michigan, Illinois, and North Platte Rivers, along with Willow Creek, Moose Creek, and Indian Creek, were veritable moose-heavens. Ask any fisherman who has tried to cast his line into any of them. And, while at it, ask Jim, the wildlife biologist.

With the technical analysis out of the way, I then undertook the task of public involvement. I set up meetings with the ranchers who ran cattle on the forest by permit. Almost to a person they objected. Innocently, I asked, "Why?"

"Moose will compete for food with my cows."

"Moose will destroy my fences."

"The government is already ruining my life. This is just another invasion of my rights."

It seems my supporting evidence—letters and statements from ranchers who lived in moose country in Wyoming, Montana, and Idaho—carried little weight in changing local minds. I was "the gov'ment" and I was trying to put ranchers out of business. Already on the verge of bankruptcy—as they perennially claimed to be—they would go broke "fixing all the destroyed fences, and the cutbacks in permitted cattle numbers, due to the overwhelming loss of forage, due to moose competition." Never mind facts.

Writing the Environmental Assessment turned out to be easy. I had met with ranchers and let them have their say. I listened. I included their concerns and refuted them with facts. I even included mitigating requirements, such as the DOW would pay for fence repair due to moose damage. The State didn't like this, but we all knew this was a red herring

I scheduled a public meeting to discuss the results of the EA, the backup for the decision document. We reserved the church basement, large enough to hold a crowd, which was normally hard to muster for anything in this small town. I wrote out all the steps of the analysis on large flip chart paper and prepared to give the opponents all the benefit of doubt. The night arrived, along with the Forest Supervisor and Jim. I introduced myself and all our bureaucrats, the first time most locals had met the Supervisor.

The more than sixty residents who attended sat listening patiently. I was pleasantly surprised at this large a crowd. There were very few interruptions or even questions. I was thorough and I think I surprised many who thought we were just trying to ram this project through. My conclusion was to recommend approval by the Regional Forester of the project but with a few stipulations to address the ranchers' concerns.

When the evening was over, the spokesman for the opposing ranchers, a gentleman named Frank, came up to me, shook my hand, and said, "I still don't like the end result, but by damn, at least you listened to us and I appreciate that. I can live with your decision." I hope my jaw wasn't dropped as he turned and walked out. I don't know what more can constitute success than such a comment.

The Regional Forester signed the document and the Division of Wildlife went into high gear to bring in moose. They had already made an agreement to trade the State of Utah moose for sage grouse or something like that; nothing as glamorous as moose, but something Utah wanted. They also started working with Wyoming to supplement the expected herd in the future. Any successful transplant and introduction of a species needs genetic diversity and the State was thinking ahead.

The DOW had been waiting for years, so it acted fast. Keep in mind that the fall and winter of 1977 was a serious drought year. So serious, there was little snow in Utah's Uinta Mountains, where the moose were to be trapped. One cold December day, we got a phone call from Denny, our State DOW contact, a notorious cowboy of a biologist who gained fame years earlier by dropping out of a helicopter while tagging elk and actually landing bareback on a bull elk before stabbing it with a sedative-filled hypodermic needle. He had been fired, spent a year or two in Africa with the Humane Society, then reappeared with the DOW as their moose expert. He said rather sadly, that the trapping had been suspended that year. Seems the Utah wildlifers had trapped a big bull moose high up on the slopes since the lack of snow had delayed the winter migration to lower-elevation, easier-to-get-to country. Salt Lake TV stations were on hand filming the rather exciting procedure when the moose slipped out of the harness holding it and fell a couple of hundred feet from the helicopter sling. The lesson learned was that moose didn't bounce very well and such a dramatic return to earth was not exactly good public relations. Wait until next year was the result.

So we waited. During that year, Denny arranged with producers of the "Wild Kingdom" television series to film the release for an episode. I learned one day in October that Marlin Perkins himself was sitting in the local café with Denny. DOW had been putting up a sturdy rope netting along Michigan Creek to hold the moose as they were released. This two-acre enclosure would hold the moose for a week to imprint on them that this was home (fig. 5) and don't wander too far off for a while. I thought this a good idea, but my bureaucratic upbringing threw up a red flag. They needed a special use permit for the filming. I went to the café, introduced myself to Marlin, and said "hi" to Denny. I then sheepishly asked if they had gotten a permit to do this filming. Marlin said nothing, but Denny rather arrogantly said they didn't need one. I knew they did but didn't press the issue. Why throw any obstructions in the effort, which had been delayed long enough? I drove up to Michigan Creek, where the enclosure was already erected and appeared that it would work well enough. I climbed a tree next to the road and realized this was a good perch for photographers and bureaucrats as well. It was a large tree with great branches close to the ground.

We waited. It was snowing in Utah, as well as Colorado, so the trapping started. One morning I came into work and found the office deserted. I asked Lonnie where everyone was. She looked at her fingernails and said rather meekly that everyone was out watching the moose being released from the truck.

"What??" I almost screamed. "Why wasn't I notified? This has been my project for two years!"

Lonnie looked at me, trying to stay calm. "I don't know. I had a note on my desk when I came in. Dave just said he got a call at 3 a.m. that the moose were on their way. He said he had to be there. Didn't mention you at all. I guess I assumed you would be there, too. I'm sorry."

Just then, Marty came in the back door and wanted to know what the screaming was about. He was the timber staff and knew that Dave and I didn't always get along. I almost choked as I stuttered, "That sonofabitch didn't tell me the moose were here. He didn't even let me know. They are out there now."

"Let's go," was all he said as he pulled my arm. "Got a camera?" he asked as we rushed out the back door to his green vehicle.

"Hell no. Why should I have brought one."

"Don't you have an agency camera?"

"Hell no. Dave wouldn't let me buy one. Said I didn't need one for my work."

"What, mother of mercy, did you do to Dave? He must really hate you. I have two cameras. I said I needed one for timber sale admin and he said to get two."

"Dirty rotten sonofabitch." I was fuming as Marty calmly pulled out of the parking lot and raced down the highway out of town.

"It's still your project, you know," he drawled that North Carolina accent. "I know somehow you will get the last laugh on this."

As we pulled onto the Forest road to Michigan River—plowed two days before by the County, another fact which I didn't know—we met a cavalcade of vehicles, including a large high-walled stock truck from Utah DOW. We had to pull off the road and into a snowbank to avoid being run over. Dave was in the front truck.

He stopped, rolled down the window, and smiled. "A little late. Sleep in good?"

"You knew they were coming. Why didn't you call me?" Marty put a hand on my arm as I started to raise it in a fist. "Why?"

Dave smiled. "I got a call at 3 a.m. I didn't think they would be here this soon. I didn't want to wake you in the middle of the night."

"You sure were here, weren't you? What a..."

Marty interrupted, "They unloaded?"

"Yeah, they only brought the first four. Still trapping them as we speak. More will be here tomorrow. You need to be here at 6 a.m." He rolled up the window and drove off, followed by three State DOW vehicles. Following them was the vehicle with Marlin and two cameramen with a back seat full of cameras.

Marty and I somehow managed to get back on the road and drove on to the net enclosure. Lots of vehicle tracks and no moose in sight, although there were a lot of tracks inside and outside the rope fence. A bunch of moose tracks led on down the road and disappeared in the forest.

"I thought they were to be released in the enclosure," I muttered.

"Looks like the best-laid plans went to hell," Marty said as we got out of the truck. There was nothing more I could do here, so we stared at the fence for a few minutes, then turned around and headed back to town.

I refused to speak to Dave and he made no effort to talk to me. I learned later that as soon as they let the moose out of the truck into the enclosure, all but one cow immediately leaped over the six-foot-high fence and took off down the unplowed road. The one cow headed deep into the willows in the enclosure. Before the bulls left the area, one stood eyeing Marlin, who was posed in front of the camera and "challenging" the bull. The moose wanted no part of this and pawed the ground before starting to walk toward the TV star. (I could tell when I'd met Marlin at the café that he was not what he seemed. On TV, he appeared to be in the midst of the action in all his adventures. In reality,

Marlin was well past his prime. He could hardly move and when he did, it was in slow motion.) Pete, his assistant, dove towards Marlin and pushed him underneath the truck as the big bull charged where he had been standing seconds before. I never saw the TV episode, but I heard it looked like Marlin had stood up to the charge. They successfully deleted his rescue and the headfirst dive under the truck.

I made it to the remaining transfers to the pen (fig. 6). After a week, there were only three cows and calves still in the enclosure. The cameraman returned to film the release of the remaining moose. It was a blustery day, with snow off and on. The cameraman walked to the far end of the net enclosure and was working with his assistant to take down the net. Marty and I were to go into the north end and work towards the south open end so the moose would come out of the willows and before the waiting cameras. I was a little uneasy going into this tall, thick willow jungle. The moose had in the past week trampled down a few narrow paths through the willows, but there were walls of impenetrable willows lining the paths. We were to walk down the paths, yelling and waving our arms, pushing the moose south. Sounded good in theory. I made it to the end without seeing any animal. Marty was not so fortunate. Halfway down, I heard a yell and scream and a pounding of hoofs and puffing and snorting. The snorting was not Marty. It turned out to be momma and baby charging toward Marty. He hit the ground and covered his head. The moose leaped over the top of him, got to the north end, turned around, and headed back over Marty, still cowering in the snow, wondering if he was still alive. They kept going this time and came out and nearly ran over the cameraman, not as safe and secure as he thought. That was the last any of us saw any moose. Actually, it was to be the last I ever saw a moose in North Park.

Marty and I walked down the road after we finished recomposing ourselves. We could see moose tracks and moose droppings. We marveled at the snow fleas in the hoof prints in the snow. Marty asked me again what I had done to Dave to incur his wrath. I said I had thought long and hard and figured he simply didn't like my management style. I told Marty that the first day Dave showed up after his transfer to the District, I was having a meeting with ranchers in the office conference room. Dave stopped by on the way to his office and said "hi." A couple of the ranchers, still irate in those early stages of the moose study, lit into Dave and accused him of putting them out of business. Dave got bushwhacked, much to my surprise and dismay. I was learning how to deal with the ranchers, but he never had a chance. I think he always blamed me.

Several months later I wanted to have a public meeting to discuss travel management. We wanted to close some roads on Park Mountain. The entire mountain was crisscrossed with old logging roads, most of which didn't go anywhere and could be put to bed without causing any travel hardships to hunters or anyone else. Dave didn't think the meeting was a good idea but I said we had to try. He went to the meeting feeling lousy, in the early stages of what turned into pneumonia. He got ambushed again by irate residents who thought we were depriving them of places to drive and hunt. After a few minutes of yelling and accusing us, Dave simply said, "There is no reason to sit here and take this. I am going home. Goodnight." And he left the meeting. I couldn't blame him, but he certainly blamed me. I think those two things led to his not trusting me in anything.

After I told Marty about that meeting, he said, "Yeah, now I can see why he doesn't like you. Not fair, though. You were trying to do a good job. Don't let it bother you. You did a good job of this moose thing."

The moose were loose, but I had one more episode with the moose. A few weeks after the release, Tom the local game warden asked me if I wanted to fly with a Colorado State University researcher and DOW pilot to locate the moose. All had been radio-collared and we needed to know where they had dispersed to. I jumped at the chance. I began to wonder about the wisdom of this when the plane landed at the Walden airport. Tom said, "Here comes Barf Airlines. The DOW pilot is notorious for his dropping of fish in alpine lakes in the summer. I flew with him once and lost my cookies. He comes in about two feet above the crest of the ridge, dips down to lake level, drops the fish, and then climbs straight up to avoid crashing into the next mountaintop. He does this day after day."

"Good thing we are not dropping fish," I meekly replied.

"Yeah, but to do the survey, he flies a grid pattern at treetop level. You know what that means?"

I didn't, but soon found out. Tom didn't fly with us that day so Sam the post-doc student sat in the front seat next to the pilot, working the antenna for the range finder. We circled around the area to start and couldn't find a single moose. I happily sat in the back seat unfolding the forest map so I could mark where we saw the moose. I knew the area and was thrilled to see things from the air. It was a new world for me. Lots of snow, lots of trees, but no moose.

"Hang on back there. I am going to have to go lower and fly a grid. Best way to find these critters." The pilot played with his instruments, then we headed what seemed to me straight down, earthward.

I had located our position exactly, but the map crinkled as I jolted in my seat, wanting to grab my stomach at the same time I grabbed the map tighter.

When the pilot said he would fly a grid, I quickly learned what he meant. He was now at treetop level with the forest screaming by much too close to me. He flew straight for a mile or two, then made two 90-degree turns and headed back the way we came, only a mile further east. Or west. Maybe even north. I became completely disoriented, and I began to feel very much uneasy. I looked closely at the map, trying to ignore the ground moving much too quickly for any human brain to absorb. Then another turn.

"Nothing at all," said Sam. He was busy adjusting his controls. He even opened the window and tried to adjust the antenna. He had no luck with that, so he played with the dials some more. "Don't understand why we aren't getting any signal. We have what, a dozen moose down there, all collared, and we can't get a single signal. Why?"

The pilot shrugged his shoulder, then turned to ask me, "How you doing back there? Haven't heard anything from you."

I gurgled something as I found talking somehow made my stomach churn even more.

The pilot turned even further, quickly grabbing a barf bag from behind his seat. "Here, make sure you use this if you need it." I held the bag, praying it didn't come to that. Yet, somehow I felt I had to use it or else die. I hoped the death would be quick. I had never felt more miserable in my life. I had given up looking at the map. Or outside the window. I was staring at my feet until I didn't even recognize them anymore. Closing my eyes made things worse. Was there anything to do or look at or think about to somehow bring my body into some kind of balance?

I was fading into early death when the pilot said, "Damn, we will never find them. Let me go way high up and see if we can expand our vision."

Did I hear him right? Maybe death could be avoided after all. We flew almost straight up for what seemed an hour, then leveled off. I could see half of Colorado below. I felt better. No barf bag yet.

"Bingo, got one," yelled Sam. "Two, three. What are those guys doing way up there?" He pointed to the north, miles from where we had been flying. "There are four. Man, they have really flown the coop. They've traveled miles. Look down there. I see one. Two."

"Let's go up there for a while. Hey, back there, are you getting these on the map?"

I think he was talking to me, but I wasn't even on planet Earth by this time. Or above it. I did feel better, but I was praying nonstop to land. The hell with the map and the moose. Who cared where they were? They were in Colorado. That's all I cared about.

I don't think I blacked out, but I lost touch with anything else going on in that plane.

I did perk up when I heard the words, "Okay, let's head down. I think I have the info I need." Was that Sam, or maybe an angel? I might live after all.

We landed a few minutes later. The pilot unbuckled himself, Sam opened the door and motioned for me to exit the plane. I fell out, probably as green as the grass by the runway.

The pilot turned and patted me on the shoulder. He looked in the seat and smiled. "You made it okay? Good job. Last week I flew with Tom and when he got out, he told me not to pick up the spare helmet in the back seat. He used that instead of the barf bag. Damn landlubbers. I just told him to keep the friggin' helmet. I wasn't going to clean out his breakfast."

It was amazing how quickly I felt better, but I thanked him and wished him a safe flight back. I fought back the urge to say I never wanted to see him again. I loved to fly, but this wasn't flying. This was a medieval form of torture. I wondered if Dave told him to do this to me.

No, I knew this was pure scientific research. I'd love to take this pilot on the ground doing a transect through the willows.

Five months later, I transferred off the District. I never again saw a moose in either North Park or Colorado. I did hear from friends that two years after the release, the moose had expanded into areas we didn't think they would reach until 1988. I also heard that those ranchers who had so strongly opposed the moose introduction had found these lovable characters so appealing that they adopted and named individual moose. They also opposed the hunting season, not wanting their pets to be shot. Go figure.

Moonwalking

Exhausted from dealing with controversies—satisfying no one, finding enemies and opponents every way I turned—I decided to do something fun: I created a program of 'hikes under a full moon'. The idea itself was not new, but for the Forest Service to sponsor something a little out of the ordinary and not try to sway public opinion in the direction of multiple-use, was new. At least for 1996 in the Black Hills—the founding-father-land of multiple-use, home of the very first National Forest timber sale, where it is difficult to get more than a few hundred yards from a road anywhere on the forest.

Though inspired as a spin-off of a program on the Medicine Bow National Forest, there was no budget for it. Needing something light-hearted and fun after struggling through a year of furloughs, strangling budgets, and low morale, I decided to just do it.

My goal for the program from the start was to have a good time, with an interpretive angle at a very low-key level. I wanted to offer a variety of opportunities for a variety of people. Some walks would be easy, some more difficult. I would not try to sell the Forest Service or the agency mission. I could work in a few things to say about what the Forest Service does, but I didn't want a hard sell. Just being there in uniform would give a very positive message. There would be no controversy over forest management; we would be seen as sponsoring something for the community that was fun, showing the public that we were neighbors. I also had another goal: aiming for the local community as our audience. I would not target recreation visitors in the summer as is often the case with many interpretive programs.

I advertised via a news release: "A Moonwalk—Hike Under a Full Moon." It would take place on the new Roughlock Falls Trail in Little Spearfish Canyon. I received help and encouragement from fellow employees at the Black Hills Visitor Center; it happened that they led that first Moonwalk at the end of June since I had to be out of town. The first Moonwalk was a resounding success. Over 200 people showed up. This caused last-minute improvising by Lois Zieman, who graciously agreed to be in charge of 'my' first Moonwalk. She broke the group into two groups and was able to retain the Native American storytelling theme.

The next Moonwalk—at the end of July—was scheduled for Crow Peak outside Spearfish. This was a different crowd than at Roughlock Falls (an easy, level, handicapped-accessible pathway). The Crow Peak trail is a three-mile hike to the top, gaining over 1500 feet in elevation; the narrow trail often through rocky terrain is not for the faint-hearted. This got the attention of my boss; his comment was "what about safety? The Deputy Forest Supervisor has expressed concern over people getting hurt." No mention or thanks for the success of the first Moonwalk, just a bureaucratic roadblock. We compromised with a start time of 5:00 p.m. in order to reach the top of Crow Peak in the daylight, then hike down as it got dark. A sunset walk would be fine; at least the moon would be out by the end of the hike. In the news release, I emphasized safety during the hike; flashlights and water were recommended.

A local historian volunteered to give a short talk at the summit on the history of the area. I realized the hike would be well attended when I arrived at the trailhead at 4:30—thinking I would be the first there— and over two dozen folks were waiting. The hikers quickly spread out— each going their own pace—and many of these paces were faster than I could keep up. Within the first few hundred yards, the 125+ moon-walkers were well dispersed.

The presentation on top was scheduled for 8:15. By 8:00, it seemed the entire group was on top and getting restless. So I had the local history buff begin his talk as people ate their snacks. He finished as the sun was setting at 8:30. People were starting to mill around as I gave them two choices. The official program was over and people could start down if they wished. I was going to share two Native American stories for those who wished to stay. About half the group headed down. After I read the stories, a young man approached me and said he knew the stories—he was Lakota and had heard them many times from his elders; I felt like an amateur lecturing to a professional, but he said I did a good job.

As the light faded and the moon started to take over in the lighting department, the remainder of the group started down, although a few lingered to watch the lights of Spearfish, far below. I waited until I knew everyone was safe, then I started down. In what turned out to be probably the highlight of the entire Moonwalk program for me, an elderly woman was just arriving at the top of the trail. She was 80 if she was a day—your typical little-old-lady-in-tennis-shoes. She smiled at me and quietly said, "I guess I am the last one up." I congratulated her and said that was fine—she made it and that made me feel good. She said she lived nearby, and she and her husband always wanted to climb Crow Peak; because he was dead, she was doing this for him. Her family was waiting on top, and I needn't wait for her, she was doing just fine, thank you. Looking at her and the sad look on her face, I was holding back tears. As I started down, several people were waiting for me so they could ask about her. I said she was doing just fine, thank you.

The walk down turned out to be in the dark, but with the amazing light of the full moon. It was invigorating; the moon took on a new dimension three miles up the narrow, rocky, often steep trail, far away from the comforts of streets and houses. People I met on the way down were having a good time. I went from one group to another and I thought I was meeting the same hikers, but didn't know them at all. I learned one facet of this type of hike that I found very enjoyable: you could walk with someone and talk with them without knowing who they were or even being able to clearly see them—sharing an experience that was ripe with discussion topics. While standing talking to one group, another came down the trail to where we were standing. As they reached us, one woman tripped on a rock, making a full butt landing at my feet. She quickly got up, laughed, and merrily went on her way. She didn't mind, and I found that no one had any bad thoughts or negative experiences, even with a few bumps and thumps along the way.

As I neared the lower Crow Peak trailhead, I met two separate groups coming up the trail. They knew about the Moonwalk but wanted to get the full impact of the moon, so they were starting late. One group even knew me—as they approached and I stood there in the dark, they said, "Oh, you're Jake!" I figured they could see my uniform nameplate, but even then, it surprised me.

A few days after the challenging Crow Peak walk, we offered a repeat of the original Roughlock Falls walk as an alternative. This was attended by over 100 people—on a Wednesday night. Again, we shared Native American storytelling and again, we had to divide into smaller groups. I went as a participant, and Amy of the Visitor Center led the hike. The moon played hide and seek with wispy clouds but came out in full view as we neared the end. The majesty of the moon lighting up the canyon cliffs added a wonderful dimension.

I went into the Moonwalk program not knowing what to expect, and it evolved into a brief introduction, walking or hiking or skiing to a specific point (letting people set their own pace), then, I or a guest gave the planned presentation, and then everyone returned at their own pace and time. The second Roughlock Falls walk had proceeded at a very slow pace to accommodate everyone. It felt like a slow-moving line at a movie theater. But people need to walk at their own pace; some move quickly, some slowly. Forcing everyone to follow a slow-moving pace was not comfortable. The moonwalk format differed from interpretive walks and this slow-moving experience changed my mind about using the Moonwalks as traditional interpretive hikes.

I learned a lot of things from these initial moonwalks, particularly when I asked people why they liked the hikes. A typical answer was that it gave them comfort and company to do something they didn't feel they would ever do on their own; most people would not go out and hike Crow Peak by themselves at night. They enjoyed doing it with others, even people they didn't know. Some liked it being family-oriented; they could take the kids. Some liked the talks, some the scenery, and some the feeling of just doing something different. Succeeding in a challenging experience develops a bond among participants. For many, they would probably not hike to the top of Crow Peak. There were many people from Rapid City; this required an hour drive, 5-to-6 hours on the mountain, then an hour back to Rapid, returning after midnight—that is commitment! Several women came by themselves. I asked why. Their responses were interesting: they would not think of doing this by themselves, their husbands would not do it with them, they sought the adventure, and they found safety in numbers.

I wrote a press release about two weeks before each Moonwalk and faxed it to local newspapers and radio/TV stations. This was also sent in the office e-mail to all Forest Service offices in the Black Hills, and we received good support from Forest Service administrators.

Support from local media was very good. Early in the Moonwalk series, I was interviewed on the live noon news program at KEVN in

Rapid City. Buoyed by the success of the Crow Peak Moonwalk, I was excited by the prospect of my first live TV interview. The station's studio reminded me of a cluttered warehouse, although the set was attractive; initially, I sat on a stool behind the camera and gained insight into how a TV broadcast works. The noon program anchor, Ms. Silvernail, had given me very little in the way of a briefing and suddenly called me up to the desk during a break in her broadcast. She said she would talk a little about the Moonwalks and ask me questions—then we were live. Midway into the interview, I became conscious that I was swinging back and forth in the swivel chair and probably looked like I was on a carnival ride—but I didn't stumble, or say anything outlandish. The interview went well—for the handful of people who likely saw it.

One of the local TV stations did an introduction to their nightly weather segment with a "Hey Mike, what's the weather?" video of local children asking the weatherman what the weather would be. I asked to do one before the Crow Peak Moonwalk; I stood in front of the Forest Service office with our sign behind me and asked Mike what the weather would be for our Moonwalk the next evening. Being rather flippant and probably ignorant at that time of what a Moonwalk was, Mike responded with a snarky comment about Michael-Jackson-type moonwalking, as he 'moon-walked' backward in front of his blue-screen weather map.

I also did a monthly taped interview for the Deadwood radio station. As with the TV noon news program, I had never listened to or seen the program I was now part of. It went well, and soon, I was on good terms with the disk jockey. This monthly report on the Moonwalk became routine and I received positive comments from co-workers and others after hearing me on the radio.

I arranged with Western Heritage Company of Encampment, Wyoming, to make enamel pins with a Moonwalk logo. This idea came from the Medicine Bow experience, with a different pin and logo each month. One logo and pin seemed appropriate for our program. Jackie Twiss, a graphic artist (and wife of the Forest Supervisor), designed a logo showing the silhouette of a canyon under a full moon. This logo was also used on a brochure showing all Moonwalks and their dates for the next year. We sold the pins to help pay for future speakers.

Over time, I discovered the program needn't necessarily have anything to do with the location. For example, the bat program could be given anywhere. I incorporated other agencies, landowners, and experts in the area into talks. We used a state park, a local private educational foundation, as well as local Forest Service expertise. Additional hikes after I left the program involved National Parks, the Crazy Horse Memorial, and the City of Deadwood.

To keep the Moonwalks on a weekend night, we scheduled the August hike on a Saturday, with the full moon 4 days away. We hiked along the Little Spearfish Creek fishery trail, and Oscar Martinez, one of our wildlife biologists, gave a talk on bats and bat biology. Even though the moon lacked the effect of being full, his presentation was a big hit to the seventy-some people as he had a sonar detector that caught bat sounds. The crowd was all "oohs" and "aahs" as he shined a flashlight on the swooping bats that we could only hear in the dark.

Bear Butte State Park was scheduled for the September Moonwalk, a significant Native American sacred place in the northern Black Hills. We planned to hike to the summit, as at Crow Peak. Near the end of August, a wildfire raced up Bear Butte, burning nearly all of the Park. Worse, it burned many of the steps, water bars, and parts of the trail itself. The park Superintendent said we would have to cancel, but recognizing a once-in-a-lifetime opportunity, I pleaded with him if there was any way we could salvage the hike and use it to interpret fire ecology. He thought about it and said okay—we couldn't hike to the top but could go part way. Carolyn Sieg, a fire researcher with the Forest Service Research Station in Rapid City, helped us with the talk. Over 100 moonwalkers showed up, despite cloudy, cold, and windy weather. We split into two groups and went on different trails. Our group didn't see the moon, but the other group did get a glimpse between clouds as the moon rose over the hogback ridge. A reporter from one of the Rapid City TV stations accompanied the trip; I was told this was the lead story that night on the evening news.

The October Moonwalk was scheduled for Mt. Roosevelt near Deadwood, with Dr. David Miller of Black Hills State University the featured speaker. An expert on the history of the area, he was writing a book on the history of the National Forest. The walk was to be on Saturday. I was in Billings, Montana for a week-long conference on

Interpretation. The meeting was scheduled to end Saturday afternoon, but I planned to bug out at noon and race home (a five-hour drive), in time to reach Mt. Roosevelt.

I woke up Saturday morning to a snowstorm pummeling Montana. At 9:00 a.m., one of the conference leaders went around to the various break-out groups to recommend people not check out, since the roads were rapidly closing and airports were shutting down. I quickly checked out and hit the road. I carried a cellular phone (still a new experience for me) and called home when I was on the road. Rachel said it was a total blizzard in Spearfish, the Interstate was closed (actually the entire state of Wyoming was closed). She was already getting calls on whether we were going to cancel. I had to get home to make this decision, although I did tell her she could decide for me.

Unable to get into Wyoming on I-90, I turned off at the Little Bighorn site and headed on a back highway toward South Dakota. As I turned off the interstate, I found the road was open but unplowed. I had no choice, I had to continue. Vehicles going the other way covered me with slush and I found the windshield wipers barely worked. Reaching Belle Fourche just north of Spearfish, I found it had hardly snowed there. Maybe things would be all right after all—then I realized my folly. As I drove into Spearfish, I understood the full force of the effect of the Black Hills on the weather. In the eleven miles from Belle to Spearfish, it turned into a full raging blizzard. The Forest Service office was just off the interstate, and as I pulled into the parking lot, I immediately became stuck. I abandoned the vehicle, but who could tell? There were vehicles stuck and drifted-in all over the place. I called Rachel to come to get me; she just barely made it in our four-wheel drive. Of course, there was no concern over the Moonwalk. I didn't have to cancel it—Mother nature did. No one could drive anywhere, and to the residents of the Hills, every sane one understood there would be no Moonwalk that night. Our first cancellation.

Thus began the winter-from-frozen-hell in South Dakota. Blizzards and cold were the norm until April. However, we continued the Moon-walks! The decision to make the Moonwalk program year-round, at least through 1997, proved challenging in the winter of 1996-1997. Winter crowds fell to less than fifty, but the Moonwalks continued to develop a good reputation. They caught the attention of the community and many people who never hiked one still made positive comments about them and showed support. We stayed non-controversial, avoiding topics dealing with forest management or anything that had shown controversy in the past. The program did not require any budget; an hour or two a month of my time was the only cost to the government. Most of the time that I spent on the actual hikes themselves was donated. I didn't want there to be any reason for anyone to try to discontinue the program.

November was scheduled for the Vore Buffalo Jump, an archeological treasure-house west of Spearfish past the state line. It was subzero temperature, but we seemed to be getting used to that in late 1996. There were calls on whether to cancel; I stoutly said "No, we advertised this as rain or shine and I at least will be there. I went out to the site in the afternoon and found the wind chill was cutting and there was fresh snow. "This is Wyoming," I thought, "and people expect this weather." We had twenty-five hardy souls show up, under a cloudy sky. Gene Gade, an Extension Agent from Sundance, Wyoming, and a member of the Buffalo Jump Foundation, gave a very good talk. I missed most of it as I had to play parking attendant to guide latecomers. A highlight of the evening occurred when another member of the Foundation Board was reading an essay by a Native American author; the full moon was almost peeking through a thinning of the icy clouds, and a flock of geese flew overhead, honking in the dark. Their calls made the entire group feel at one with everything, including the spirits of the Lakota, the buffalo, and the geese. I played my wolf howls tape, the howls echoing through the foggy night; the effect on the group down in the massive pit was almost as good as the geese. Almost—the geese were real.

The December Moonwalk was scheduled for the 23rd. I was nervous because a week earlier, another blizzard had shut down highways, with wind chills of 40 below zero. It made the thought of any outdoor activity rather ridiculous. Weather forecasts showed maybe a break from the relentless snow and cold. I decided to go for it, as it seemed to be a good time to discuss the scientific and astronomical explanations of the Christmas star. Potential speakers were either going to be gone for the holidays or didn't feel qualified to speak on this subject. So, I located a book that I could use for reference myself (a minister in Belle Fourche loaned me his copy), and I researched the subject and felt prepared to briefly discuss the Christmas Star theories. Then, over the weekend, another foot of snow. I went to the site on Sunday afternoon to do a dry run. The snow was deep, partly crusty, and very difficult to walk on. Obviously, we couldn't hike very far, but just a little way and we could be high enough to see the holiday lights of Spearfish immediately below. 'Rain or Shine', remember?

When I left my house, bundled so thickly I could barely move, the thermometer read 20 below. We still had 15 people show up, walking bundles of fur, down and insulation. I had to refer to my notes, which I could see with the flashlight Rachel was holding. I hurried through it, talking with numb lips and cheeks and teeth. I had no feeling in my toes by the time I finished. Everyone enjoyed it, and appreciated the new brochures for the 1997 Moonwalk schedule; we then all climbed up the short hill above the interstate, watched our frozen breath for a few minutes, and dispersed. When I got home and had almost warmed up, I received a phone call from a gentleman in Sturgis who was angry because he couldn't find us. As if it mattered, I tried to explain where we had parked and walked; he was genuinely upset that he missed the walk.

By this time, I was starting to turn over the program to Amy, who was considered the primary Forest interpreter. I had decided to take an early retirement come summer and wanted to ensure the continuation of the program. So January found the Moonwalk on her turf on the Pactola District out of Rapid City: an Icewalk on Sheridan Lake. She coordinated with a group of fishermen to talk about ice and ice fishing. As usual, it was zero or subzero, but crystal clear. I was mainly an observer, but continually mingled to get the group of three dozen to move around, cognizant of the problems of frozen toes and noses. The talk was very good, with "oohs" and "aahs" listening to the lake ice boom as it did its mysterious expansion game. The ice was over a foot thick and certainly solid, but it was still an eerie feeling being over several feet of water with a thunderous cracking going on under our feet.

February ended my active participation. This would be a Moon-ski. Deer Mountain ski resort hosted our group on their groomed Nordic ski trails. Amy planned most of the details and arranged for a wildlife biologist to talk about winter wildlife. Needing to be familiar with the terrain and details of where to go, I checked out the resort a day ahead of time. As I turned off the highway onto the road to the ski resort, I hit a slick spot and ran off the road into a deep snowbank; no damage, but I had to chain up to be able to move again. I skied down the trail a little way, just enough to know where to go in the dark. (Getting back into the vehicle, I realized I had lost my personal keys. Luck was on my side; I found the keys right away, in the snow as plain as day at the scene of the chain up.) Nearly fifty people showed up on that frosty night for a good, but somewhat short ski. I missed most of the talk by the biologist as I helped a novice skier who just couldn't keep his skis on his feet; we limped in as it ended. Everyone enjoyed themselves, and once again, the reporter from KEVN in Rapid City attended and we made the evening news.

March was the first Moonwalk I had no part in. Amy took over and had a walk along the shore of Pactola Reservoir. It was a cloudy night and the speaker from the Weather Service was not as engaging as other speakers. It was the night of the eclipse and showed promise since it was also the time of the Hale Bopp comet. The clouds would not cooperate until after the hike; according to Amy, she stopped on the drive back to Rapid City to observe the eclipse among parting clouds. She said the turnout was good, but not over fifty.

Mt. Roosevelt was rescheduled for April. Dr. Miller was dying of cancer but bravely agreed to try to do the program, with Mitch Mahoney, a Forest Service archeologist and good friend of Miller, as backup if needed. April 1st found the never-ending winter continuing to pound the Dakotas as it dumped two feet of snow amidst howling winds and bone-chilling cold. I knew we would not get within five miles of Mt. Roosevelt by the time of the Moonwalk two weeks later, so we traded places with the May location: Ft. Meade Recreation Area near Sturgis in April, and Mt. Roosevelt in May.

As April advanced, snow had changed to rain, and the night of the Moonwalk saw a steady cold rain. Rand Smith, a living-history authority on Dr. McGillicuddy—famous frontier Army doctor and Indian agent—gave the presentation. Less than a dozen wet and bedraggled adventurers showed up. We huddled under umbrellas listening patiently to Rand give his presentation, and then hustled back into our cars. What a shame, since there is so much history at this frontier Army fort.

At the Crow Peak Moonwalk, I had announced a photo contest for pictures taken during the hike. Two people submitted photos that I enlarged for display at our office. Earlier, I had planned the September 1997 hike for Old Baldy, another 3-mile trek through many stands of aspen. The program was to be a local photographer giving tips on nature photography. I was retired and living in Colorado by that time, so didn't see how it turned out.

The Moonwalk program seemed to gather a life of its own. By the spring of 1997, it had spawned several look-alikes. Devils Tower National Monument asked us to help them do one at the Monument in August. For a visit by the Chief of the Forest Service and other dignitaries, the Nebraska National Forest did one east of Rapid City in the spring of 1997 to celebrate National Grassland Week; theirs competed with one of our regular ones, but it still drew a small crowd. I led a mini-version of one for a regional "Interpreters' Workshop" held in Deadwood in May. As part of the multi-day event, we would climb through the Mt. Moriah cemetery above Deadwood, where lie Wild Bill, Calamity Jane, and other frontier legends. As the bus unloaded the fifty participants, the skies opened up with lightning, thunder, rain and wind—not conducive to walking on a hilltop.

May—third try for Mt. Roosevelt. Dr. Miller had passed away, and Mitch dedicated the talk as a memorial to his mentor and friend. I had decided this was my for-sure final Moonwalk, as I was taking early retirement in a few months and the Moonwalk program now belonged to Amy.

It was one of those rainy-one-minute, sunshine-the-next, type of days. A furious thunderstorm hit the area at 5:00 p.m., and the sky cleared at 6:00, in time for our hike at 7:00. I drove up to the parking area to see about twenty cars already there; people kept coming. The skies stayed clear. By 6:30, I was visiting with many of the almost 100 people already there. When we started at 7:00, over 100 enthusiasts were gathered, ready to begin hiking up the hill. I gave my usual introduction, including the safety message with a caution about lightning, invited everyone to stay after the talk for a campfire, thanked them for coming, and asked about Moonwalk regulars. I discovered I had "groupies"—a few folks had made nearly every Moonwalk, certainly a feat considering the abominable weather the last six months. I barely got past the lump in my throat that this was my last Moonwalk, although they would continue without me. I was given a round of applause, then we started the short hike up the wide path.

At the top, Mitch gave a very informative talk on the unique stone memorial, one of the hidden secrets of the Black Hills (fig. 7). Built under the urging and assistance of Seth Bullock, former sheriff of Deadwood—Teddy's buddy in the young and turbulent days of conservation—few people know it is there. Then, one of my co-worker's sons lit the prepared campfire. About half the people stayed to enjoy the camaraderie. What a nice touch I thought, for me to end my Moonwalk career on. About that time, a clap of thunder immediately overhead caused us all to look up. Our clear sky had suddenly clouded over, and the skies opened up. Everyone was immediately drenched; lightning flashed directly overhead. We headed to the cars a quarter mile below, but there was no use trying to stay dry, nor was there reason to be mad. We were soaked and thoroughly enjoyed the moment—laughing and reveling in our communal misery—sloshing as we walked. What a way to end it, I thought, as I looked through rain-covered glasses, and laughing, spit water.

I returned to Mt. Roosevelt the following morning to think about my last moonwalk—what a way to exit, with one of the best things of my entire career. It was quiet at the memorial. The crumbling tower dedicated to Teddy Roosevelt juts out of the youthful ponderosa pine forest. I smiled as I sat briefly in the same location in the warm, drying sun. I cleaned up the remains of the campfire and picked up the few candy wrappers left behind. Locked to prevent anyone from climbing inside the tower, it presents too much danger of someone hurting themselves and suing the government. Somehow that itself is a sad commentary on the difference between the days of Teddy and now. Teddy would have huffed and scoffed at sissies who could not enjoy a little spot of danger.

But the previous night there were more than a hundred people who likely would have applauded Teddy and wished he were here. They took a step towards the courageous by hiking on this moonwalk—all the moonwalks required a little courage. Going out into the night, in sub-zero temperatures, to a foggy sinkhole buffalo jump haunted by Lakota and bison spirits, to a frozen lake, to the top of Crow Peak, and along a bat-infested streamside—to find themselves and test their spirit of adventure, all in the company of other adventurers. That is what life is about, at least to me. And certainly was to Teddy.

I unlocked the cable across the gate to the tower and climbed the unrailed stairs. The air was cleaned by last night's ozone; the sky was crystal clear. Teddy would have enjoyed this. The forest obscured the view—he would say we need to cut some for sawlogs. He would be right. There is a right way to manage and a right place to do it. In my career, I have seen both done right and both done wrong. That was the past now and I had turned down the road to my future.

The Forest Supervisor was thrilled with the letters he received in support of the Moonwalk series. He assured me he would continue them after I retired. I reflected on what I accomplished: I didn't ask anyone's permission to do them; I made a decision and followed up on it. It took initiative I should have taken on things twenty-five years ago. But, no, I realized—I had tried the unusual during my whole career, and that was probably why I gained the reputation I did. A little weird, a loose cannon, a liberal in a very conservative outfit. (It started in 1971 when I posted a notice at the trailheads and campgrounds along the Conejos River that I would lead a nature walk to Conejos Peak on a Saturday. The only feedback I got was a sneer from my co-worker Charlie: my printed notice said I, the assistant Ranger, would lead the walks—he crossed out the words assistant Ranger with a big question mark. No one showed up for my walk and Ranger Tom never said a word, in support or ridicule.) But through the subsequent decades—all the field trips with schoolkids, the newspaper articles, and the open houses in Del Norte and Teasdale—when no one else thought the educational ideas worthy, I tried them, usually with minimal agency support. But I tried.

The stone tower rose above the trees. Its presence showed a desire to try something different, something honoring an ideal. It was past its prime, decaying in forgotten glory. Was that my career? So what if it was? I stood still and looked around. I was alone, with only weeks to go before heading south to my retirement home. There was a lot of reflecting to do. A lot of Moonwalks, field trips, news releases, and new ideas tried that I would have a lifetime to reflect on.

The public loved the Moonwalks. They thirsted for a chance to have fun, without controversy that surrounded everything else the Forest Service did. I think they were as tired of the fights as I was. Hasn't this been the story of civilization? Humanity can't get past the idea of enemies and distrust of people with different ideas. Wouldn't it be great if we could all stand by a campfire on a hilltop as the clouds open up with rain and lightning? That would put us all on an equal footing, relying on each other.

I heard a chickadee calling from the trees behind me. As I looked for him, I saw a fleeting glimpse of a doe leading a spotted fawn across the small opening into the dark forest. Must be brand new, since this June day was early for fawns. Good luck, kid, you will need it. I think we all need luck, as well as hope, about now.

A Pair of Farewells

To my favorite people:[1]

The time is here to end my first career; it's early retirement. It's time to turn out the lights and walk out the door into the sunrise of a new career. For months, I've thought about what I might say when this time came, but now the time is here and it's difficult to find the right words. All the words of wisdom, the accumulated knowledge, the lessons learned and forgotten—all disintegrate in the breeze. Such is history and such is the need for all of us to make our own mistakes.

I am sending this to friends I've had the pleasure and honor to work with over the years. Those years have stretched beyond several horizons and fade away into a past that is so different than today. That may be one of the lessons. Times change, things evolve; we who work with the environment and ecosystems know that. Most of my peers are slowly graying, part of a generation that arose in the sixties and seventies. We had our day in the sun and I've found the sun has set on my career. I did my best, as we all have done. Many of us share the old stereotype of the person who would rather sit on a lonely hilltop and watch the sun slide behind a cloud low on the horizon. As we have done this, the world has changed beneath our feet. When we joined this agency, we wore white hats. The Forest Service was the pride of the government fleet of bureaucracies; we were honored in our communities.

Well—something has changed. I am not ready to try and describe the what-and-why. All I know is I don't care to continue to work in an agency and with a public I don't understand anymore. We were born in the upheaval of the environmental revolution as well as the sixties idealism. We came in to save the earth and we did a pretty good job. But the world changed; we did too, but I guess I did not change enough. Now

---

1   Written in late July, a few days before retiring, and sent to Jake's private list of Forest Service people.

I sit here blinking away the confusion like a lost hobbit wondering why forces of evil are invading his peaceful hobbit hill.

Like a warrior returning from battle, I am weary of the wars: fighting ranchers over grazing rights and over-used range, the wilderness and RARE II battles, spotted owls, forest plans, skunks and porcupines, moose, and cutthroat trout. This list goes on and on and there seem to be no victories or defeats, just stalemate after stalemate. I am tired of fighting the good fight, trying to follow the good road. I see the old generation slowly fade out and the corporate history and pride fade with them. Not to belittle the newcomers—their dedication is sincere. But it's not the same. Part of the change that happened while we were watching the sunset was the public we were trying to protect. They became greedy, they became noisy, they became unfamiliar with how we lived and thought, but most of all, their world changed for them, too. The West and its public lands are in a revolution and we have yet to sort out where we all fit. So now we are caught in the din of conflict, of confusion, of a situation where quite simply, there isn't enough to go around. And we have leaders who cannot—or are not allowed to—lead. And direction that doesn't direct but floats around like smoke.

Most of you are not far behind me, although I am leaving about 4 1/2 years earlier than planned. I wish you the best and hope you can keep this leaking ship together. I have my doubts about the future of the agency as we knew it. It will change even more and that's your challenge and concern. Guide it well. My hope is soon we will re-gain leadership and direction, for that is what I see as the biggest reason we are adrift. But I'm not sure that simply doesn't reflect society as a whole. You deserve better. I, as a soon-to-be general public, applaud you and say thank you for an often thankless job. I have not thanked the people who work for me nearly as often as I should, and feel like I haven't been thanked as I think I should. We all need support, now more than ever. Each day, thank someone for what they are doing or trying to do.

My hope is the agency will not only practice ecosystem management but understand what it really means. To me, it is captured in a quote from Kipling;

"There was never a king like Solomon, not since the world began.
Yet Solomon talked to a butterfly like a man would talk to a man."

When we take the time to appreciate—and yes, talk to—a butterfly, then just maybe we will realize the sacred trust we have in treating this land with the respect it deserves. And when we do that, just maybe we will treat each other with the respect we deserve.

And so I turn out the light and leave the Forest Service. But the Colorado Rockies, the Sierra Nevada (fig. 10), the Utah plateaus (fig. 9), and the Black Hills will never leave me. They—and you—will always be a part of me. A part that I plan to put in writing and may be calling on you to share a few memories. In the meantime, keep me informed on what is happening. I can be found watching the eagles soar in front of a crimson sunset (fig. 8) over the North Fork Gunnison River valley.

To the Universe:[2]

The early August night was sweltering hot under the sky of the Lakota. It felt right for Deadwood on the first Saturday of the Sturgis Rally. There were motorcycles everywhere. Bikers and biker chicks wandered the Deadwood streets—up and down and back again—searching for adventure, excitement, and themselves. Or possibly escaping from every-day lives, finding a fantasy they wished they could live, even if for only one week or one night.

For whatever reason, there they were. And there I stood, waiting for Travis to find where he parked the car and pick me up as I stood in front of the restaurant, holding my retirement party treasures from this special August evening. I had just said goodbye to one life. Goodbye to a career that ended the day before. Goodbye to friends, most of whom I'd never see again. But more importantly, to a career that started with such hope decades before, now ending on an uncertain note. As I'd said in my fare-well a few days before, I had just turned off the lights and quietly shut the door. And what an appropriate way to do it: I walked out the door, into the Deadwood night and joined the crowds in their meandering search. My main regret was Rachel was not here with me, a silent companion

---

2   Written a week after retiring—after his retirement party.

and support for all these years. But she was already at our new home, forced out of our home, sold much sooner than expected. I joined her late the next day, in the southern Rockies, to begin our new life.

The 'good-bye' night wrote new memories: Kelli in a dress and stepping up to assume her new role. Tony and his botched story—that's okay, Tony, we knew what you meant. Mitch and Zig with their Nookies candy bar prizes; would they bring good fortune? Mitzi swinging her biker whip—you are safe with Galen, but what do we tell Luke? Tom, my frustrating reason for early retirement.

All stories end when the torch is passed to a new generation, a fairy tale with many endings. This generation I said goodbye to wasn't new, but one step behind me. The agency of the late nineties lacked a new generation. That was one thing that was wrong. Years of budget cuts, political interference, a changing of society in general, all combined to change the organization beyond recognition. Colleagues left and were not replaced—their work farmed to remaining staff—a trend that was breaking many spirits. I now belong to the group of people who spin yarns about how things used to be. And things are different, as they are to the elders of every generation. When I joined the agency, I ignored the old-timers who told us how it used to be before these college-educated-idealists came on board to change their world. It was as if I walked by a library and didn't even look inside. Now I realize I should have looked or listened, but it's too late. I had my time, as they did theirs.

My job had been simple. Protect our environment first. Second, use natural resources for the good of society. After that, the jobs overlapped and intertwined into a web of controversy. I started out not knowing or understanding any of this. I was young, green as the trees I lived and worked amongst, and naive about most things. I started slow but gained speed as well as understanding. I saw old ways of doing things that didn't evolve with our understanding. I fought the system all the way, losing most of the time. But I made small changes. More importantly, I began to see and hear and think about right and wrong, about the importance of our place in this web of life. Did I make a difference? Questions like that went beyond a night like this. They were what philosophers from Socrates to Nozick pondered; there were no answers, but looking for them occupied their time and their energy. I would think not of the big picture but of the small things. The aspen stands outside Del Norte struggling to stay alive amid the maturing spruce overtopping them. The coyotes of Boulder Mountain evading the airborne trapper shooting at them. The streambanks of Sierra Valley surviving the over-logging by frantic bureaucrats. The last grizzlies of the San Juans. The alpine forget-me-nots. The peregrine falcons, moose, mountain bluebirds, and cliffs of Conejos Canyon. The memories welled up with the tears.

This was the last in a frustrating series of assignments. My entire career consisted of trying to escape a bad assignment. Only to get another bad assignment. I couldn't focus on advancing any career. I was too busy trying to walk sideways, not forward. The luck of the draw? Or was it me? Probably both. I was not cut out for playing the game. I was always fighting rules I didn't like. Fighting for opportunities to work with people I respected and admired. Sometimes you draw several bad hands. Sometimes you only get a few hands. If they are all bad, well, that's the game.

I arrived in Spearfish not wanting to be there. But it was an escape. I didn't fit in. When I got there, the team was already in place. They were the younger, yuppie group in a plum location. I was an outsider, but more importantly, I was burned out. Like a dog that has been kicked and abused, I had lost my spirit. I was going through the motions. I liked the previous forest and district, but was caught up in big-time politics. You don't win when you fight the Forest Supervisor. I did a good job and accomplished things I will always be proud of. But I got burned and I escaped with something missing inside me. So, the people in Spearfish didn't know me. I had no more fight left. My heart was in Colorado. I had wanted to return to Colorado ever since I left it years before, but never quite made it. My home would be there from now on, but never again would I call a piece of it my district. There would be no more districts. Others would carry on. I'd had my chance. Now it was gone. I appreciated the compliments, the jokes, and the kind words of the people at the party. But I felt sad they only knew a small part of me. It wasn't a part that was my best, but it was all they knew. I wanted to tell them I was better than they had seen for the past five years, but at this point, what did it matter?

I tried to look at the night sky, above the Deadwood lights. I tried to look beyond the Hills enveloping the famous town. That same night sky that was here before Calamity Jane, before Custer, before Crazy Horse, before the forgotten generations of Cheyenne, Lakota, and their ancestors. We are all newcomers, not really understanding what history means. I couldn't concentrate on what I wanted to; that is what I need to explore about my career. The things that happened were too many people, too much noise, too much selfishness, and not enough understanding of who we were, where we lived, and how we lived. I started this part of my life that was now ending, thinking of how I could save everything under that night sky that began far to the south, under the stars that lit the Ute and Apache sky. Same sky, same stars, but hovering over something far different than now. I will have the rest of my life to figure all that out. What mattered was I tried and now it is someone else's turn.

At some point, we all fade into the night darkness. I faded into the night, then early next morning, faded out of the Black Hills. I and my overloaded truck—looking like a Clampett-mobile—uneventfully journeyed to the land of my forever dreams. And there I sat, amidst boxes and a jumble of a lifetime of possessions, both real and imaginary. As we unpacked the boxes, I could not help but sort through the memories as well. Each took a turn with my attention, and each was a meditation. Memories. And stuff. Life is made of both.

Ready to start my new life, as I drove up to my property on the mesa, I watched an eagle jump from a power pole cross-arm and slowly soar over a field, seeming to lumber like a heavy cargo plane. Off to circle in his search for adventure, as well as his search for food.

I also saw a new sight on the mesa. A lone coyote watched me from our neighbor's prairie-dog-infested field. I'd heard him many times before, but never had I seen him mid-day so close. He turned and trotted off as I drove up to him, with a glance back at me—with an arrogant yet playful smile. I barked at him. This caught his attention, but he only paused before seemingly rolling his eyes, as if to say "humans!"

Both the eagle and coyote had been here in the prairie-dog-cafeteria, catching late afternoon snacks. Both are content every day to wander into the night and morning sky in search of nothing more than getting through another day.

The clouds hid the horizon as rains soaked the high country all day and much of the previous week. The fog played along the mesa and poured over the rim into the Black Canyon. Mt. Lamborn was like a pile of whipped cream—puffs of blue and gray clouds with only a hint of mountain. Everything seemed to be hiding and searching. Changing in color and mood. And so did I. It was time to go back to the rental house and unpack another box.

Part I Photo Gallery

Fig. 1: "...Rio Grande National Forest, Conejos Ranger District...." (p. 6)

Fig. 2: "I lived in a cabin by a river in the mountains, got to ride a horse, and worked in my very own wilderness of trees and streams and elk." (p. 7)

Fig. 3: "...National Guard...building duck ponds, blasting rock cliffs, and building roads." (p. 5)

Fig. 4: "... develop more water for them so the cows could better use all this allotment." (p. 9)

Fig. 5: "This two-acre enclosure would hold the moose for a week to imprint on them that this was home...." (p. 16)

Fig. 6: "I made it to the remaining transfers to the pen." (p. 19)

Fig. 7: "...one of the hidden secrets of the Black Hills." (p. 35)

Fig. 8: "...watching the eagles soar in front of a crimson sunset...." (p. 40)

Fig. 9: "...the Utah plateaus...." (p. 40)

Fig. 10: "...the Sierra Nevada...." (p. 40)

Part II

THE UTAH YEARS

Jake's Introduction

Written during my four-year assignment in southern Utah,
I've kept these five essays separate from all my other writings since
I'm not sure I want anyone to read them. I was venting my frustration
with the local culture. I had a good idea of what I was getting into
when I accepted the assignment, because earlier in my career when
I had applied for a job in Mormon Country, I was cautioned by the
decision-maker that a non-Mormon needed to go into the community
with open eyes. I was told that a non-Mormon might not fit in, that the
culture in rural Mormon communities was different—parochial and not
always welcoming to outsiders, especially to Gentiles as we were called.

Most assignments in my career were in small, rural Western towns. I
call them pioneer communities; if a person's parents and grandparents
were not descended from the pioneers who came West in the mid- to
late-1800s, they were considered an outsider. Even people who had lived
in the community all their lives were sometimes considered outsiders.
Add in the factor of religion, such as in rural Utah, then it's doubly
hard to fit in. I have no problem with the religious differences. I feel
"everybody—each to his own." And that applies to politics, religion, and
general philosophy—as long as it doesn't hurt anyone else.

What made it more challenging in rural Utah was the recent history.
Settled in the time of Brigham Young, Mormon settlements in Utah
and other parts of the West carried a certain obligation to the faith.
Transportation was difficult, the terrain was rough, and people were
self-sufficient. Wayne County was no different. There were no good
roads into this isolated area until fairly recently. In the few years before
I arrived, several highways were built or improved which allowed the
outside world to find it. For example, the Boulder Mountain highway—one of the most scenic drives I have ever encountered—and
the road to Hanksville, were only recently paved. The residents of the
county had lived all their lives without much interference from the rest
of the world. By the time I arrived, tourists were discovering the scenic
wonders and liked them. Environmental groups realized the scenic-
and geologic-tourism potentials of this area; many thought the entire

area belonged in national park status (fig. 11). The locals were used to thinking of the national forest as their backyard, to do with as they saw fit; that included continuing their way of life cutting timber for their little sawmill, grazing cattle like their granddaddies grazed, and hunting for meat to survive. I came along thinking my job was to manage the national forest according to federal laws, which didn't fit with local customs; I was an outsider trying to change their way of living.

After a while, I was branded an 'environmentalist', which in their minds, was equal to calling me a communist, or worse. We started getting threatening phone calls at home. Rachel, who taught art in the local schools, was branded. We both bought pistols and practiced shooting. Is it any wonder I've had negative things to say in my writings? When friends in other parts of the country asked how I liked it in Utah, my response was: "the land is amazing, it's a wonderful place to work; the people, however, leave something to be desired." It turned into a love-hate relationship for me. I always felt that given time to adjust, the people part of the equation would level out. Maybe it has by now, thirty years later. Maybe I came at the wrong time; I hope that was the case.

If these essays are sarcastic, a little negative in tone, then I apologize. But I wanted to capture something difficult to explain. I don't know if they will ever see the light of day. If they don't, then they were therapeutic writing them. Judge for yourself.

The Dog Who Started the Great Utah Coyote War

Occasionally I sit alone, surrounded by the emptiness of meadow or forest, and contemplate the moon, especially a full moon. A false emptiness as it turns out, when it is pierced by a coyote's mournful song—by the song-dog of legend and fable, hated like the devil and worshiped as the master of cunning. You are not truly in a wild place until sitting alone you realize are not alone after all.

Walking away from the flickering campfire, I gazed into the night sky above an unnamed meadow on Boulder Top, the cathedral of southern Utah. Our annual Fourth of July escape from civilization brought us to this remote hideaway, surrounded by emptiness that causes one to reflect on just about everything that has happened ever since apes fell from the trees and discovered they had toes. The full moon added to the ambiance of this setting. So did the singing of the coyotes. First, the one wail, then the chorus as others caught the rhythm.

The song of a coyote is a stimulating sound. Not really frightening—more primeval than anything—it is fully representative of the freedom that we all wish we had, a freedom that is in the mind and not any freedom of actuality. It is not the absolute essence of that feeling; that belongs to the wolf. I've never heard a wolf howl in the wild, only recordings. To me, the song of the wolf is the most absolute heart-rending, mournful sound ever created. I cannot help but feel that it is the sound one would hear if you could rip your heart and soul from your body. It is the essence of the wilderness; it represents wildness and everything tragic about what we have destroyed in nature; it is the soul of man that has been lost through civilization. It is the ultimate, only mimicked by the coyote song. Coyote song serves as the wolf stand-in, since very few humans are lucky enough to hear wolves in the wild.

Hypnotized by the moon, counting stars and tracing the silhouette of the spruce forest against the darkening blue-black sky, I heard the coyotes. I pretended they were wolves. And I dreamed and mourned, as one has to do in this situation. It is something in our makeup, in our genes. Listening to the lonely cry, then the growing chorus of yips and yaps, I thought of the unbelievable predicament the song dog had gotten himself into. Especially on this mountain. My mind wandered to the recent history of me and coyotes.

The coyote serves a very natural, very necessary role in his environment. As long as that environment pretends to still be natural in any form, the coyote as a predator is a critical part of the system. Upset one component of the system and you play havoc with the entirety. Many ranchers and ranch sympathizers cannot grasp this simple fact of life. Mention coyote and you have the rural redneck reaching for his rifle: the only good coyote was a dead one. Of course, they gave lip service to the right of the coyote to live, but not within their range of vision. A hungry coyote had been known to eat a sheep or two. Even been known to kill for guts and glory, to bask in a Charles Manson-like glory of killing for fun, quite possibly for the sole purpose of driving ranchers to bankruptcy. Many folks in the county, and in many similar counties across the West, genuinely hate the coyote. They teach their offspring to shoot them for fun.

The Utah Division of Wildlife supported coyote killing on the west side of Boulder Mountain, to keep the antelope population from growing. Coyotes like to eat baby antelope; maybe the local coyotes read ecology textbooks and figured out predator-prey relationships. Meantime, the antelope herd over the past several years had expanded and started to cause problems usually associated with overpopulation (i.e. lack of food, etc.). And sheepmen were realizing that antelope might be effecting the sheep forage. True enough. Cattlemen on the west side of Boulder Mountain had been complaining for years about too many antelope, although no one had convinced me that antelope compete with cattle since the two don't eat the same things. Anyway, why try to figure this out with logic? Logic in this and many other instances did not cross the borders into Wayne County, Utah.

So—at that time—coyotes on and around Boulder Mountain were widely hated and had been without friends until about 1990. Then, as if they wanted to widen their disdain in the West, the neo-environmentalists adopted old-man-coyote as their latest cause, and they started asking questions when they learned about ADC. Animal Damage Control, a division of APHIS (an acronym of the U.S. Department of Agriculture) existed to help farmers and ranchers by pretending they lived in a non-natural ecosystem and tried to kill animals that ate other animals or plants that had economic value. Coyotes, bears, raccoons, even starlings. ADC did serve a purpose, but over the years, it became the case of being in bed with your client. ADC took its role seriously and became the corporate killer, not asking any other questions than "where and how many?" A one-sided bias that tended to shoot when a rancher cried foul. No questions asked. All of a sudden, questions were asked by others not agreeing that a sheep should feel safe and sound when living in the home of an animal that eats such things as sheep (wild or domestic) for a living. And regardless of how much (or how little) one sheep might be worth, it was worth whatever it cost to protect it.

My involvement began when I was assigned the task of writing the environmental assessment (EA) for predator control on the ranger district. This was a normal, rather routine thing that had been done in the Forest Supervisor's Office (SO) in the past but was shifted onto the districts that year. Well, I did the public involvement thing. And I got several replies that sided with the coyote. Reading the tea leaves, I realized that the times 'they were a-changing', and maybe we should start slowing down the unrestricted predator control of the past.

The EA was written, and approved by the SO to include a triggering mechanism for ADC control. This was a difficult thing to pin down, but I had checked with ranchers and asked them what level of loss they figured was acceptable (as if any is really acceptable). Most agreed that they planned to lose about 5% to coyotes and other causes, so the EA said there would be no predator control until losses occurred and approached something near 5%. This would not prevent any coyote control, but symbolized the value of a coyote as a natural segment of the system.

Another small restriction in the final document slipped through unnoticed. The Forest Plan specifically stated that only offending animals could be killed; aerial gunning, which occurs in the winter when sheep are not on the range, was not acceptable, as it embodied the philosophy that the only good coyote is the dead one that gets creamed while bursting its heart trying to run from a chasing airplane, rifle pointing out the window. Does that seem fair from any civilized point of view? It did to ADC and ranchers. But not to a growing number of people who realized their tax dollars were being spent to do this. Figure in economics and it would have been enormously cheaper to give the sheepman the cost of every sheep eaten by a coyote rather than spend five times the value of sheep killed by coyotes in order to kill a few coyotes. Do you know how much it costs to fly an airplane for an hour? Do you want to compare that to the cost of a sheep?

The decision was appealed by the environmentalists, not by the sheepmen (although they did complain and grumble). It seemed to me that the latter weren't smart enough to play the appeals game. This may be a harsh judgment. That's not necessarily bad, but it is unfortunate if you value a fair fight; this fight really wasn't fair. The Southern Utah Wilderness Alliance (SUWA) and its allies had money and smart lawyers—and public sympathy. Lots of people now knew about the physical beauty of southern Utah and were willing to give money to save it. The sheepmen and their allies were not sophisticated in the litigious ways of urban society; until they learned to play the game, they were bound to lose, both in court and in public opinion.

In this instance, I truly felt sorry for the locals. They were content to continue living the life their grandparents lived. Unfortunately, the world was changing around them.

The decision was upheld, but I figured this was round one. Round two came in the fall, and the Forest officials—not liking the ranchers' complaints—decided that maybe aerial gunning was a necessary thing to do since the agency did want sheep grazing the range. And those poor ranchers were destined for bankruptcy if the coyotes kept it up. An EA, written in the SO, was hurried through approving gunning after all. No mention that it overturned our earlier decision, no public involvement to speak of, and quite poorly written if I may say so. Nor was there any mention that it violated the Forest Plan as written. Subsequently, that second decision was overturned on appeal, with many red faces in the halls of the SO. At about this time, someone realized the real problem lay in the Forest Plan. There was suddenly a need to change that to make it easier to bow to the will of ranching community.

I noticed the moon had moved across the sky. The coyotes had stopped singing and my dog Varda lay asleep by my feet. The campfire had died to embers. My mind returned to the events that set the stage for my becoming the 'Coyote Pariah of Utah'. Varda and I started the ball rolling "to put every sheepman in Utah out of business and destroy ADC." Pardon a little braggadocio. Of course I really didn't have anything to do with it, but at the time I saw every sheep look at me with hatred in her eyes. I was marked; quite unfairly, because I like to eat lamb and bought one every year from a local sheepman. Funny how irony creeps into these complicated issues.

It went like this. All that fall, I had been exploring the Bureau of Land Management (BLM) canyons behind our house. An old trail was marked on the maps as starting near Sunglow Campground and climbing the cliffs to the canyon maze east of town. I had been locating this trail and marking it. It had not been maintained for years, but at least it was used enough on the flats to easily locate. I saw other tracks on it and occasionally saw local kids on bicycles leaving town and riding toward it. The point is, the trail was right outside town and was used.

On New Year's Eve, I went for a hike on this trail with my recently adopted pup. I hadn't been on the trail for over a month, but the day was warm, and I wanted to take her out. She was a recent rescuee from dog pound death row, and she continued a long tradition of family hiking dogs (fig. 12). I needed to introduce her to the active life of hiking and being outdoors on and off trails.

To my surprise, there was now a small sign on the trail warning of poison and traps ahead. I picked up Varda and carried her until we reached the rocks; I realized the local trapper wouldn't walk this terrain, so I set her down and we continued up the trail. A nice hike actually, as we explored the red rock canyons on that warm winter day.

On our return, as we came off the cliffs, we hit the trail about the same time a trap hit Varda. She went berserk with pain. I don't handle panic well, especially as a dog is sinking her teeth into my arm. I was trying to figure out how to open the trap and at the same time keep my arm from being torn by slashing dog teeth. Blood (all of it mine) was flying; fur was flying, and the trap was flying, with dog and dog foot still in it. Finally, I opened the trap and got her loose, but both of us were in pretty tough shape. I was not thinking kind thoughts at that time. Who in their right mind would put a trap right in a trail that is next to the town that has kids using it?

I carried her back to the truck, but on the way, I discovered right in the middle of the trail, closer to town than the trap, was a coyote-getter—the nice little device that shoots cyanide into the mouth of anything that would grab onto it. Mostly coyotes, but also family dogs, or even a kid who might grab it out of curiosity. I had walked over this, not seeing it, on the way up the trail, and miraculously had the dog in my arms at that point; she would be long buried by now if I had let her walk earlier. I didn't need this to infuriate me even more, but somehow, I did reach a new level.

Upon reaching home, I called the local ADC trapper. Luckily there was no answer, for if he was, I'm convinced one of us would be in jail today for homicide. I'd met him a time or two; he was a strange character, without a sense of humor. At that moment I had no sense of humor myself and I also had a feeling that an intelligent human being did not exist within the confines of ADC.

The next day, I called the ADC office in Richfield and tried to ask in a civilized manner why cyanide and traps would be placed in the middle of a trail so close to town. The die was cast.

The trapper soon was let in on the incident and he called to tell me he was removing all traps and that "the blood of all local sheep would be on your hands." I told him I wasn't asking him to do that, just not put traps or cyanide right in the trail with inconspicuous warnings. No matter. He was removing the traps and telling everyone it was my fault.

I immediately called one of the local sheep ranchers I respected and explained that it wasn't my intent to stop all coyote control, and I wanted him to know the facts of the incident.

Soon, my dog and I were famous. Of course, word got back to me that ADC called me a liar: there were no traps or cyanide on a trail that close to town. It didn't take much in this community to be branded an Environmentalist; anyone who sided with coyotes was of course a capital E enviro; I was out to get the sheepmen and ADC. I wouldn't be surprised if my dog and I had been discussed in the halls of Washington; my Forest Supervisor certainly was aware of the episode.

Well, after that, the coyote battle escalated. The Forest Plan was changed, and appeals ensued. SUWA carried the so-called pro-coyote crusade to Washington and it seems the general public started to question the continued existence of ADC. From that point on, district staff were removed from any decisions concerning the matter—it was all S.O. level and above. All future controversy in the minds of Wayne County held me accountable. I was pro-coyote, thus a snarling menace to the continued existence of life as they knew it in this seemingly peaceful southern Utah community.

For some perverted reason—to me—this made the moonlit song of the coyotes on Boulder Top all the more sweet. Poetic justice or something like that. Let the coyotes thrive, let them eat all the children of the church-going, God-fearing ranchers. Too bad I couldn't push for the introduction of wolves. No need. The coyote has to be admired for surviving after hundreds of years of persecution.

There is some philosophical lesson in this, too. The noble wolf, the top of the line, somehow didn't make it. Just like when the golden age of Greece during its pinnacle of civilization failed to survive while the barbarians did survive. Doesn't seem right. The aristocratic wolf disappeared but the wily, cunning, barbarian coyote survived. Does that foretell something about us? Are the intelligent ones of us doomed, only for the rednecks to survive? Does PBS fail while MTV succeeds.? Nix to the National Endowment for the Humanities while the National Rifle Association grows by leaps and bounds?

That's not a good analogy though. I do like and admire the coyote, if only for his place in the overall scheme of things. He is there, thus he is needed. Maybe not as glorified as the wolf (or as hated), but he belongs. And I do like to hear him sing.

I stared at the moon as it overpowered the crystal clear sky. The stars flickered as they had for millions of years. The breeze blew the embers of the dying campfire. The dog was safe for now. I was also safe for now, knowing the coyotes were out there. They once again started singing their serenade, gloating over surviving for another day. They will survive, but the world around them is changing. I think they and their proponents have turned the corner. Battles are still to be fought; times will get ugly. But the critical mass is growing. The feeling that 'everything-out-there-is-for-humans-to-change-however-we-want' is ebbing. The Pioneer West is a thing written in history, although the death struggle will go on for a while longer.

The howls tapered off and then there was silence. The stars made no sound. The moon knows the end of the story, but it keeps the secrets to itself. I crawled into my sleeping bag, wondering. By sunrise, the coyotes would be miles away, eating mice.

They Will Hang My Skin from the Courtyard Wall

THE COUNTRY BELOW THE rim of Boulder Mountain is just as magical as the tundra-like meadows above it. It is the transition from the slickrock desert of Capitol Reef National Park to the forested top of the mountain. When I sit on the edge of this no-man's land, I can gaze at the maze of red rock canyons on all sides. This would be the foremost state park of anything east of the Mississippi; here it is the yawn of boredom, worthy of no more than Bureau of Land Management status. It's just more of the same-old-thing in this part of Utah.

Since access is easy and snow cover light, I started coming in the winter to this secluded rock maze on the edge of Torrey. The mountain, brooding above to the southwest, is covered with snow. Here—with every square mile within sight different from its neighbor—it's another world.

The rock formation I am most interested in, is the Moenkopi—red-purple sandstone that forms stair-step canyon walls—stepping stone slabs with ripples and raindrop depressions giving haunting hints of thunderstorms and flash floods echoing across swamps millions of years before the dinosaurs. As headwaters of the big canyons further down-stream, silence reigns over a landscape etched with draws and gullies and canyons building in intensity (fig. 13) from here to the national park a few miles distant. Dry as sand, silent as the universe—hidden for an eternity—it is now open to the world, mute to its history.

That far-off history (as well as stepping stones for my yard), is what beckons me to the canyons and cliffs. To someone who can see, it is an open history book, just as most of this slickrock country. Unfortunately, many people choose not to see it. If they even look, they see rocks: bare, worthless red rocks. Too dry to farm, too rugged to build on. Too far from anywhere. It's just here, as people pass traveling from somewhere to someplace else. Too bad, but that's part of why I love it. It is all mine at times like this. Magnificent and desolate and sacred. I think of someone like Babe Ruth sitting alone in an empty Yankee Stadium in December. You feel the excitement of times past and enjoy the presence of the place, but you know you are only visiting memories and echoes.

I look at the cliffs and see the world in slow motion, the unbelievable epoch of time. I see a world that existed right here, in this same place we now call the United States; we now call Utah; we now call Wayne County. A world that no longer exists. Just like the worlds that created the starlight shining down from the belt of Orion in the winter sky. Those worlds are no more and haven't been for millions upon millions of years. We see the past, just as surely as we see the view from a time machine lost in a previous universe.

A world existed here in which the sun rose in the morning and set in the evening. And not a bird sang, not a mosquito buzzed, not a noise existed except the unending wind. A wind that carried the sand from far away eroding mountains. Mountains that have not existed for millions upon millions of years. A place that is no more, but instead is exposed for those who can see. It is my history book. The Moenkopi is as distinct from the Navajo formation as Florida is distinct from the Bering Strait. Each rock formation tells a story and its place in time.

To stand here looking at the rock is to see into the face of God. Whose-ever god that is, it doesn't matter. The god who created this world and sat patiently as she so masterfully made and destroyed and made and destroyed again and again. Aiming for perfection, she did just that and tossed it aside to do it again. It pales the mind as I contemplate the scale of this theater. For miles in every direction, the soul of the earth is exposed. To me, heaven will be when I can go back in time and see what this place looked like when it was being sculpted. But I digress. That's the fun of this. It is escape and it is creation and it reminds me of my humble place in all this.

It also reminds me of the blindness and ignorance into which so many of us are locked. This location I am standing in now is not far from a small piece of private land next to the national park. Land that is similar to this; land that certainly creates the same feeling of awe and wonderment to anyone who craves to escape from wherever their world is.

It is a piece of land that came to the attention of the Utah Council on Arts and Humanities, or whatever their official name is. They had a chance to buy it. The artists and humanists on this Council had flashes of forethought and brilliance. They conceived of a place where they could build a retreat. A retreat where creative people could come and escape the routine world of cities and cornfields and concrete and committees, and find their meaning and meanings of life itself.

Artists and humanists tend to want to do things like this sometimes. I know. I am married to an artist and she likes to look at nature and life and draw it. She sees things there that make her think about her own meaning. I consider myself an artist too since I like to write and create my paintings with words. And I know a lot of people like to get away from things that cause stress. When a person with any kind of open mind is allowed to use it, it does wondrous things. Such as contemplate what nature has lain out before us, behind us, and ahead of us. Nature is life and most of us aren't allowed to see it in all its raw beauty anymore. People who write books and poems and songs or draw people or landscapes do this contemplation. All these things are about life and the role of people in it. And since life can be a little complicated, creativity requires a peaceful interlude from the chaos of civilization.

So, these artists and humanists thought this retreat idea might work. They could bring creative people to this isolated piece of desert, and they could contemplate and muse and create. These same people could then share their books and songs and paintings with the neighboring communities and school children in this remote place. What an idea! What could be the catch?

Rachel and I were invited to attend a meeting in the courthouse in Loa one afternoon. A very small and select group of local artist-types were asked to come and hear what the Council's committee had to say. We went out of curiosity and the hope that there was intelligent and forward-thinking life south of Salt Lake City. Surely, this community could not turn down such a proposal, especially if almost nothing was required of the community to make this work.

The committee presented their idea to us. 'Us' included one county commissioner. He was there for obvious reasons. He represented the people of the county. He was asked to support this idea. All he had to commit or even consider, was conceptual approval. And something as simple as a commitment that the county would maintain the road to the retreat once a year and maybe plow after a big snowfall. No big expense, just a symbolic gesture, something that the county did regularly for isolated ranches in this part of the world.

Several of the Council's committee favored this location over other sites for their idea. I remember Gibbs Smith, a publisher in Salt Lake, felt the same awe I did with this country. I was impressed that we had people of his caliber and influence wanting to do something like that here. There are a lot of places in Utah that offer remoteness and beauty. Usually, there were a lot of politics involved in selecting a place like this, and usually it took a heavy-duty political pull to land something like this. With a population of about 2000, Wayne County was not known for having much political pull or clout.

The idea sank in as they talked. We could entice the likes of Steven Spielberg, Terry Tempest Williams, John Updike, Yo-Yo Ma, Jonas Salk, Joan Baez, Robert Bly, Bill Moyers. Right here in Wayne County. What an opportunity, at almost no cost. I thought this was a golden egg being given to us by the goose. I thought how could we lose?

We now looked to the county commissioner for his response. He was non-committal. I'm sure he never grasped the full meaning of this for the county—for the residents, and especially for the school children. We waited for someone to speak.

The high school principal then spoke. He (an outsider, new to the county, and a naïve gentile who hadn't yet grasped the local mentality and paranoid way of thinking), supported the idea. He encouraged it. In passing, he used the word wilderness. It was in an innocent context that could be interpreted as: this unspoiled environment that deserves awe and protection from what has happened to so much of the rest of the world. He meant no political advocacy; he just made the type of statement I would expect in most conversations about this red rock desert.

I cringed, recognizing immediately what he had done. He didn't know he had 'yelled fire in a theater'. He never realized he said the word 'wilderness'. That word in this very conservative community carried more emotions and baggage than just about any other word in the English language. It 'threatened' and challenged the survival of this community and lifestyle. It reeked of liberal hippie freaks who chant the mantra of Wilderness with a capital W.

The Titanic was hit. The damage was done. The boat started sinking. The discussion then entered a whirlpool that sucked intelligence out of the room as surely as the bathtub drain sucks out water.

The Commissioner grasped the 'real' meaning for the county, for the residents, for the school kids, and for the future of their way of life. The retreat idea would bring in intelligentsia and radicals. It would bring in 'environmentalists'. It would bring in ideas to local folks he was elected to protect from fire-breathing satanic-worshiping-enviros who were out to eradicate honest god-fearing people who were placed here by Brigham and his disciples to protect Zion from said types.

In his slow drawl, he spelled out his analogy to this plot: the story of a local politician in a small Texas town who was in cahoots with the bad guys. When the townspeople found out, they did their righteous best and strung him up in their courthouse square and hanged him up to dry for all the locals to see and learn from. "By God," the commissioner said, "I will not forsake my duty. I will not be a traitor to the good people of this county. If I were to okay this or even carry it on to the full commission, I would be strung up just like that poor fellow in that small Texas town. They will skin me and hang my hide from the courthouse wall. I am here to protect this county from outsiders who are trying to take over our way of life. I will have no part in this scheme. We know how to live our own lives and God is on our side. We will have no part of this plan to corrupt us and our children." Or something like that.

The idea withered and died then and there. We walked out of the meeting stunned as if we'd just seen a real-life dinosaur emerge out of the Moenkopi. Actually, I had witnessed a dinosaur, a brain-dead relic of a civilization that devours its young in order to protect them. I felt sad, I felt enraged. But in reality, I was not surprised.

The committee left town. I think they understood. Wayne County had a reputation, and they saw why. They didn't try to convince anyone else; they never came back. They had given us a chance and we turned them back at the border with our sticks and stones and firebrands. I heard later that they did fund a retreat near Zion National Park. But thank God, it was not in Wayne County. The citizenry was safe from the knowledge of the outside world. Safe from ideas and knowledge that ways of life can and should be challenged and debated.

Lost in thought, staring east toward the private land that could have housed a secluded retreat, my gaze returned to the red sandstone at my feet, sculpted by ripples and fossilized raindrops. My mind conjured up ducks and dinosaurs and the shores of distant oceans. The pockmarks on the rocks at my feet reminded me of the Pleiades and millions of stars throwing photons at us from the far side of the universe. I could hear the shifting sands and the rippling waters that existed here in the morning of time. I heard symphonies yet unwritten by Bach or Yanni or Bernstein. I read the poetry of Shelley and McKuen and writers yet unborn. I understood the work of Steven Hawking and the elusive unified theory. I saw the universe expand and return to the Black Hole that ends time and starts it over again.

Clouds were floating east over Boulder Mountain. They formed shapes mimicking the rock; they too, are novels and symphonies. The mind of God is at work here, revealing secrets hidden since the beginning of time. If only a person was given the serenity and time to discover this, I mourned. I just sat silently and listened, lamenting the beauty that goes unseen, letting it drift on over the canyons. Does Pericles now weep for the lost glory of Athens? Does Jefferson mourn the lost ideals of his country? Do the poets of Alexandria cry for the books lost forever in the flames of hatred and ignorance?

I do think our minds in fact play tricks on us. They have a lock that must be opened. Creativity has a price. Only a select few know the combination of that lock. Too many of us wake up every morning and spend the day waiting for the next—not thinking, not challenging ourselves, nor our leaders. We do not know how. We must look for the lock and seek and share the combination to open it. Once it is open, I think the horizon must look like this I see before me. The ideas come streaming in. The horizon stretches forever and the light sparkles like diamonds. The twisted junipers are stewards pointing the way, and the rocks hold secrets to questions we haven't even begun to think of.

Must we continue to live in ignorance? Evidently. At least for now. I see a hawk fly over in his never-ending search for mice. The gnarled junipers stand sentinel in the red soil and rock; winds have curled snow in a small drifts at their feet. The rocks stair-step down into the draw, each ledge an artistic masterpiece. The sunlight has melted a few pockets of snow. The water trickles down one ledge onto another. Slowly, at a pace that tests the patience of time itself, drip after drip after drip carves a new groove in the cliff.

The winds and rain slowly dissolve this rock. They have for millions of years and will continue to for millions more. We will come and go.

We will bring in poets to write their stories. We will write the songs, paint pictures, and probe all the secrets that exist. Maybe here, maybe somewhere else. But the sun still rises, the wind still blows, undisturbed by our creativity or lack of it.

I get in the truck and head back to the highway. I pass by a crumpled Coors can tossed into a rock crevasse. I will go back home and turn on the TV. Maybe I will read tomorrow night. I am just too tired tonight to think.

Chokecherry Point

THE CLOUDS OF THE fading July thunderstorm headed past the Henry Mountains to the east. Below me unfolded the panorama of desert and slickrock. Above me, the desert sky emerged as the blue that must have been brightening in intensity since its creation over four billion years ago.

I'm sitting on the rocky promontory called Chokecherry Point, the northeastern extension of the island-in-the-sky called Boulder Mountain. It is an island as surely as if it stands in the middle of the Pacific Ocean—although water of such magnitude is only a dream here. Boulder Mountain, bounded by basalt cliffs, the capstone of the Aquarius Plateau, sits majestically at 11,000 feet, surrounded by the haunting expanse of southern Utah. From Chokecherry Point, I can on a clear day see the La Sal Mountains on the Colorado border, over one hundred miles away.

Not this day, though, at least until the storm made its journey past the Colorado River, and beyond Grand Gulch and Natural Bridges. Assuming the storm lived long enough. Desert thunderstorms are as fascinating as the desert they brood over. They have a life of their own and are as unpredictable as a March wind. They provide life-giving rain, in the fast-paced fury of their birth, violent life, and peaceful death.

Chokecherry Point is similar to other places in this part of the world, usually called Lands End: Lands End on Grand Mesa in western Colorado; Lands End in Canyonlands National Park; Lands End of the West Elk Mountains southeast of Grand Mesa. How many others? They all mean a sudden end of a mountain or plateau, and guarantee an eagle's view of wild immensity beyond. There are many "lands ends" on Boulder Mountain itself. Each time you stumble through the spruce forest to reach the edge of the plateau top, you will draw in your breath in a sudden gasp (fig. 14), having discovered a panorama unequaled. At least since the last time you saw nearly this same view from a slightly different angle. Nothing is boring about hiking the rim of this flat mountain top. That's why it is magic to me, and to a lot of other people who have discovered this place.

That is part of the problem. Sort of like when God shared his creation with Adam. Surely he must have regretted it almost immediately; he no longer had control. And all those newcomers quickly started screwing it up; doing what he didn't intend. Is that what is happening here? Not that I equate the residents of Wayne County as having anything resembling the insight or aspirations of God. But things are happening that disturb them. I am somehow in the middle of this and am feeling the disturbance. The fury of the just-passed storm symbolizes the fury going on in the valley hamlets below this mountain; there live innocent, naive people in an isolated world.

It was peaceful up on the Point and I wanted to enjoy it for a while longer (fig. 15). The smell of fresh rain brightened the air around me. Not only the smell of rain and ozone, but the very air itself was alive. I remember one other time I felt this same brightness.

One day in June 1970, I was part of a National Park Service crew surveying a water line on the North Rim of the Grand Canyon. A wild springtime thunderstorm had just passed by, and, having finished our two-day assignment, we were driving back to the South Rim. I remember watching the scenery as we drove out of the forest and into a meadow. It seemed clearer than I imagined possible. I felt I had the vision of an eagle. Everything was like crystal; everything glistened. A basic scientific explanation would say something like: "the lightning cleaned the air of all dust pollution and the air was indeed clearer." I'll buy that. Whatever the explanation, it was like a whole new dimension. My eyesight is not that good and sight is one of those things that I would change if I had the power to go back and tinker with a few genes. But sight at that moment was a gift of the gods. It opened a whole new dimension.

I had not again experienced that type of crystal-clear vision until those few moments on Chokecherry Point. Typically, haze tends to obscure some of the distant views. But this moment was different. The Henry Mountains started to glow in the sunset. The canyons and domes of Capitol Reef National Park to the east were alive with color. I could count the individual pinyon trees near Bowns Reservoir. The world was below me. I surveyed it from the throne of the heavens.

Nearby, columbines almost danced among the boulders on the cliff's edge. I tried to count the different lichens on the basalt—green, light green, gray, black, flakey-gray, orange, red-orange, flakey-green, white—but couldn't keep track. Just like the tints of the columbines—light-blue to almost ghostly-white, not the brilliant blue of high Colorado Rockies' columbines. These are pale cousins, but just as breathtaking, especially with the few remaining rain drops slipping off nodding petals onto still-steaming rocks.

Why can't people agree on what to do with such a fantastic country? Anyone with a sense of ownership of this frail planet surely can see the beauty and appreciate the need to protect and revere a view like this. The lives of the people down below revolve around their earthly religion. Every little town has a big new brick church: Church of Jesus Christ of Latter-Day Saints, "Visitors Welcome." Occasionally I've considered walking into one and saying "Hi, I'm a visitor. A doubting Gentile, but a visitor to your house just the same." Would I be welcomed with open arms? Not if they knew me. Why not? Here lies the tale.

Trouble was brewing down in Paradise's hamlets. A world falling apart for these descendants of hardy pioneers. A lifestyle was disappearing. Invaders were infringing on a long-kept secret. Boulder Mountain and southern Utah were being claimed by the rest of the world. It was a fight for ownership—not legal ownership, that was stolen long ago from the Utes. Moral ownership. Maybe even survival.

I liken it to the following: the early pioneers came west, usually in search of economic freedom. In this area, it was also religious freedom. Brigham led his believers to the promised land and they thought they found it. In other parts of the West, settlers found their individual paradises in valleys from Montana to Colorado, Washington to Arizona. They found what they wanted and shoved aside whoever got in their way, with government sanction. Lakota, Kiowa, Comanche, Ute, Salish, no matter.

Well, guess what? Nowadays—across the West—a new breed of pioneers is discovering the golden West. The gold is not in the ore but in the scenery and vast open spaces. These pioneers are finding spiritual freedom. Economic freedom seems to be wavering, and god forbid, religious freedom is in trouble, too, as someone forgot to lock the gates and the Gentiles are pouring into Zion. And who is in the way? Those same folk who sing praises to their ancestors for braving the wilderness. They are being pushed out, just like their great-grandparents pushed out the Ute. And they don't like it. I'm sorry if my only reaction is, "How does it feel? Not much fun, huh?"

This situation is happening all over the West. Troubled times loom. There are other scenarios given here. A fight over economics, jobs versus the environment, states' rights, local versus federal control, and, various forms of destiny. It is complicated, no doubt about that. That's also part of the problem. There are no easy answers. It gets to the root of government as practiced in these here United States. It's the growing pains of the evolution of policy established in the 1800s, when the West was wild and free—and so big that no one ever thought we'd reach any kind of limit to its use.

Utah happens to be nearly 90% U.S. Government-owned. Between the military, Park Service, Forest Service, BLM, and other assorted agencies, there is not a lot of private land in Utah. Not as much as in, say, Illinois or Ohio. Thank goodness it's not much like back East. But that's for another reason. You don't grow much corn or beans or anything else out here, other than rocks and scenery. But you don't have the slickrock and the canyons in Kansas either. Seems to be a fair trade-off to me. But somehow, the fact that those folks from Kansas and Illinois have a legal say in how this rocky canyon scenery is used, and not vice versa, seems to stick in the craw of Utahns and Montanans and lots of other hardy pioneer stock in this federal-government-owned area. They do have a point, but short of a massive revolution and overthrow of the government, things are not going to change.

This may seem simple, depending on your ancestry and possibly your political leanings. If you want to stop here, that's fine. But I think it goes deeper. I see it in several more dimensions. Part of it goes to the moral and spiritual role that nature plays in our lives; and part of it to the managerial role of the federal government. That's enough to send most analysts reeling. Religion and politics enter the equation, and it's time for the faint-hearted to leave.

The spiritual role: you can leave out formal religion, which gets too tough, but it underlies the attitude of our Mormon friends in the valley below. (Although how many of them realize that old boy Brigham actually was something of an environmentalist? That thought would strike terror into many Wayne County hearts!) I am something of a Druid myself and feel we are all interconnected. It's the Gaia hypothesis if you want to call it something. The rocks and mountains and desert are all in this together with the deer and eagles and humans. We live and breathe depending on each other. As we lose touch with nature in the raw, such as is happening in Salt Lake City and Denver and much of California and most of everything East of the Mississippi, we hold precious the wild areas that remain. We need these to go into and stand and feel the wind and the grass and the ancient stirrings of the song of the coyote. And maybe even the voices of those ancient Biblical prophets. Which is more important: a few temporary jobs that result in destruction of what you hold sacred? Or, keeping cathedrals of trees and geological wonders intact? Or so the argument goes.

The political role: it's a case of federal control. You have to start with the constitution, although many locals would just as soon as not. That causes too much internal strife since they are usually conservative, which translates into patriotism and flag-waving, as long as it is in their favor. A mistake of history or not, that doesn't matter now. No one is going to give federal lands to private ownership. Wars will be fought over that one. They were held by Uncle Sam when the states were given statehood and the states seemed glad for the deal. After all, who would ever want worthless mountains and rock canyons? They belong to the nation, which means they belong to the people, which means lots of trouble in the 21st century. How can 350 million people agree on anything?

Agreement or not, as long as 'we the people' own this mountain-and-canyon real estate, someone will have to manage it. Management comes in many forms, but it means using the land for various and sundry purposes. And more likely than not, 'various' conflicts with 'sundry' and people aren't always going to get their way. If you live in Ohio and visit Boulder Mountain, your goals of spiritual renewal may not seem much fun to the Wayne County rancher whose goal of food on the table may be in jeopardy. Jobs versus environment. Local control. How would that Illinois farmer like it if everyone in Utah could tell him how to farm his beanfields? And so goes that argument. Valid points on both sides make for endless discussions.

Why should I care, other than for poolside banter? Remember, I said I'm in the thick of it. Well, I'm one who has the challenge of managing things, refereeing the conflicts, and trying to reach compromises on how to meet economic and political and spiritual needs. All are woven tightly with emotion and that means a lack of logic and understanding.

That's why I didn't want to go down from this point once the refreshing rain stopped. The air glistened and the rocks glowed in the sunset. Orange on red, blue on green. A color explosion in paradise. Up here that is. Down there, the tone gets ugly. People can't see the mountain for the cows. They don't see the colors; they only see red. The same color as the rocks. The complexity disappears and answers seem simple. I wish they were. There is no win-win here. Someone wins, someone loses. But what do they win and what do they lose?

The Cowboys

I cannot honestly say that I hate cattle, but I can say they are not my favorite animal. Cattle are dumb, in my opinion, and they frequent many places they shouldn't be allowed. I spent much of my career working with cowboys who ran their livestock on 'my' National Forests. This has not been an easy relationship. Many of the cowboys—to their dying day—believe my sole purpose in being was to remove their cows from the forest and thus put ranchers out of business. Oh, how many times did I hear that litany?

It obviously wasn't true, but I was in many cases trying to get them to change old habits and occasionally reduce their permitted numbers or season of use. These measures were because I could not get them to spend time to put in more fences or water developments to achieve livestock distribution. The better distribution was to prevent damage to soil, water quality, and wildlife habitat. There was no compromise in many cases. If I didn't crack down, I was complicit in breaking federal regulations, and thus federal law, as well as being derelict in my sworn duty to manage the federal lands under my protection. I was delegated responsibility to manage these lands for the people of the United States and not for the individual rancher and their business profitability.

I cannot totally fault the ranchers since they were in a tough spot due to decisions made a century ago. Their ancestors were allowed to purchase lands on which to locate their base property and homes, and to graze their livestock in the summer months on the mountain or range lands that remained in federal ownership (fig. 16). Thus, they were dependent on federal land to furnish grazing during the summer so they could grow hay on their private land for winter feed. They rarely owned enough land to wean themselves of the necessity to use federal land as part of their operation. More often than not, the ranchers were allowed for generations to graze more sheep or cattle on the public lands than was healthy for the environment. It was that simple. However, as public knowledge—as well as public preferences—changed, simple facts remained: there were too many domestic livestock grazing on public land. The ranchers had no other option than to reduce their income, change their management practices, or go out of business.

On an early spring day, I picnicked in the desert of Capitol Reef National Park, and thought about cows and where they belong and don't belong. They certainly didn't belong in this National Park, in the desert of southern Utah. Maybe they belong in the grasslands of Texas or Nebraska, although I think bison would have been a better choice to graze those lands they had grazed for thousands of millennia. But that's a whole other story.

Cattle roaming slickrock desert, searching for blades of grass, is just not appropriate. Especially if that desert is a national park. One need only look at a sight like that to realize the unbelievable political power of the cowboy. The Park was formed in Congress only after significant concessions to the politics of Utah: cattle that had grazed the deserts of the Park were allowed to continue grazing. Never mind that cattle grazing is incompatible in any national park, much less one that is a fragile desert where you measure the distance between grass plants with a 30-foot tape measure, not a 6-inch ruler. Of all places on earth where cattle should not be allowed to graze are the desert washes and canyons of southern Utah. But that was the price to pay. We will all pay the ecological price of this horrendous mistake. Scenes like this did not help to moderate my bias against grazing arid country.

Cattle are appropriate up on the side of Boulder Mountain next to the Park. They are appropriate if grazed correctly. That's where I took all this personally. It was my job to make sure they were grazed correctly. On Pleasant Creek, they were not. I had spent three years trying to build a case to figure out what was wrong and what needed to be done to correct the misuse of this public land.

A few days after my above mentioned picnic-musings, I was astride Fox—a Forest Service trotter—as he fidgeted, making me fidget and adjust the saddle. Looking at the scene along Pleasant Creek made me as angry as the scene in Capitol Reef NP. This meadow was devastated; it looked like a de-graded golf course. Golf courses are an accepted practice in our society, when watered, fertilized, and carefully tended. This meadow was not. Every willow was nubbed off. Dandelions proliferated where meadow grass should have been. The stream-bank was mud, not a vegetation filter to hold back spring floodwaters. Flies dotted cowpies, which in turn dotted the meadow. The place stunk.

To top it off, the permittees saw nothing wrong with the scene. "This place looks better than it did fifty years ago." Which it probably did. But it still wasn't right.

My time on the Dixie National Forest was almost up. It was the summer of 1991 and I was putting the finishing touches on the Allotment Management Plan which my assistant Richard and I had given top priority for the past three years. The Forest Supervisor had told me: "get the management plan done for the East Slope Allotment and fix that damn overgrazing." Or something like that. I put my heart and soul into it. I had been beaten and battered and frustrated at every turn. The permittees simply didn't see any problem. And if they did almost admit one, they blamed it on the elk. Too many elk and that's why you are concerned about how the range looked. "Reduce the elk, not the cattle. It's just the environmentalists that are complaining and trying to eliminate grazing and put all the ranchers out of business."

I was sitting on Fox enjoying what I could of Pleasant Creek and the forested hillsides. It was my reward: a day out of the office in this fourth year of drought in the desert southwest. Pleasant Creek is one of the few streams on this mountain, a hidden treasure nestled on the east side of Boulder Mountain. Serendipitous was a perfect word to describe this oasis above the slickrock canyons and deserts next to Capitol Reef. And this day it was all mine as I rode up Pleasant Creek and onto Boulder Top, trying to visualize what it would look like without cattle. I could justify this day as work, but it was a pleasure for me.

As I paused atop Fox, I thought back to my history with cattle and horses. Fox was typical. He was a good horse, but he had a habit of sleepwalking. I had to be awake myself as he occasionally woke up and jumped as he realized he was being stalked by grizzlies or cougars or T-rexes. Whenever my mind wandered, he usually jumped. That's why I had to keep my day-dreaming to times when we both just sat there. His ears would tell me when he was dreaming of greener pastures, and, when he would waken and realize his peril of the moment.

I never considered myself a 'cowboy'. I tried to fit in with the local ranchers, who were the real cowboys. They knew I did not have the ranching background, thus the knowledge they had. But that was not my job. My job was to make sure they followed federal rules—as well as the science—of proper land management. They—the livestock permittees—

were one tool in range management. They made a living by doing this; it is a precarious relationship, but common throughout the West.

I thought back over two decades to my first years with the Forest Service. The stated objective of range management was to provide red meat for America's enjoyment. There was no mention of good land management. Of course, there were words in our charter to protect the land and water resources, but the production of meat was a carryover from the early days of the Forest Service—just as the production of lumber was an objective of forest management. During my career, as the public embrace of environmental conservation gained power, the agency slowly out-grew the early emphasis on commodity production. But the change was slow as we had to work through the good-old-boy-network, where Forest managers were brought up in the 'get the cut' mentality. Somehow, management of the total ecosystem—watershed, recreation, wildlife, and health of the basic elements of the ecosystem itself— seemed to fall second to getting commodities to market. By the time I was approaching retirement, holistic objectives were being recognized in practice, not just in name. But getting past the seasoned good-old-boys who were brought up through the ranks—before the so-called environmental revolution—was a challenge.

Collecting data to back up the recommendations I would make was complete: reduce the number of cattle, reduce their time spent on the more sensitive areas, and reduce the season of use. Would this negatively impact the permittees? Of course it would. This was not my objective—it was a consequence of doing the right thing: i.e. "fix the damn overgrazing."

I have heard the claim by many ranchers that they are the original conservationists. Some of them might have been, but I rarely saw evidence of it. They couldn't afford to be. In order to make a living, they pushed the limits. The health of their lands, including the health of wildlife habitat and the health of the entire ecosystem, was usually too expensive for them. As I said, they were forced into this system due to past decisions and often did the best they could.

Even though I was sympathetic to their plight, I had to do what I had to do. So...where did this put me on this day? I believe that people from Ohio, and elsewhere in the U.S. driving along the Boulder Mountain highway, might have enjoyed seeing a cattle drive moving from one mountain pasture to the next. But I also believe they would rather see a bull elk trotting across the road than a herd of cow-calf pairs.

Fox and I trotted on through the pine and aspen forest to reach the top of the mountain. There, we surveyed our own piece of paradise, even with its spots of overgrazing damage. Cattle could still graze all this, but with a few changes. The cowboys were a part of this and they did add color to an image of the old West. I wanted to work with them and keep them in the picture. Could they understand that?

Ghost Forest

BOULDER MOUNTAIN IS ONE of the 'sky island' plateaus of southern Utah. The summit of this flat-topped mountain is called Boulder Top. It rises to over 11,000' in elevation—the highest-elevation forested plateau in North America (fig. 17). Containing 50,000 acres—seven square miles of rolling meadows, lakes, and spruce forests—it is bounded on three sides by basalt cliffs that allow unsurpassed views of the surrounding country. To the east below the cliffs, it merges into the red rock canyons and cliffs of Capitol Reef National Park.

Early in the 20th century, a spruce beetle epidemic killed most of the spruce trees. For decades, there was a standing dead forest, with young trees growing up among the ghosts. After many years, the new forest was a healthy, young, almost-mature forest among the standing dead skeletons (fig. 18). For years, local residents harvested the high-quality standing dead trees for the local sawmill, which made mine props out of the still-sound wood. These were all small timber sales, usually requiring only a few farm-truck loads of trees, with no road-building required, and minimal negative impact. The high elevation forest always added to the scenic and recreational value of meadow- and lake-studded Boulder Top.

Boulder Mountain is the centerpiece of the Teasdale Ranger District of the Dixie National Forest, where I worked for four years. It is not near a large population area, thus I could easily spend a Fourth of July exploring it without running into any other people. And, as part of my job, I could drive, (or ride a horse), up there and do actual work—managing the grazing, recreation, and wildlife resources.[3]

The other resource requiring management was timber harvest. Here is a brief explanation of how that management process worked at the time: each national forest was given a saw-timber volume target to put up in timber sales each year; this target, sent down from higher levels in the agency, was based on inventoried acreage of trees and a calculated volume of trees—saw-timber-per-acre.

---

3   In Jake's short story *On the Top*, published in "Tales of Ravens Nest," he describes the effort he made to have a hiking trail constructed along the Boulder Top rim. He fought the system as well as big-league bureaucratic politics, but got the trail built.

During my tenure with the Forest Service, I found over the years that meeting those timber cut targets became more difficult. The facts were that the folks on the ground—at the Ranger District or Forest level—rarely took any land out of the acreage-base used to calculate the amount of timber available. In other words: the employees who laid out timber sales (me in a few cases) would throw out a stand of trees because it couldn't be logged due to steepness, no road access, or too rocky, but, no one would exclude those acres from the base. Thus, the Forests overestimated what timber was available for harvest, and would have to make up the difference in other areas by borrowing from the future, because the differences couldn't be made up. Over time, it became impossible to 'meet the cut'.

This was what happened with a timber sale on the lower slopes of Boulder Mountain. The district timber staff officer was showing the forest timber staff and several of us from the district, a sale where he had to delete a stand of trees because it was too rocky to harvest. I asked why wouldn't we delete that acreage from our base and thus reduce our cut. The forest timber staff officer who was present replied that we couldn't do that. I asked why. He could not give me an answer.

However, the Forest was having trouble meeting its quota of timber sales. So, the Forest Supervisor wanted to harvest much of the timber on the Top. This would be via large timber sales, with high-quality roads, something that did not exist. All of us on the ranger district, as well as the forest silviculturist, wildlife biologist, and soil scientist, agreed large timber sales on the Top were a bad decision.

The district timber staff officer had been dragging his feet on preparing an environmental assessment (EA) for a timber sale. He was in bad graces with the forest supervisor for other reasons, which eventually led to his being transferred to another district. Even though another forester was transferred to fill his position, he was reluctant to step into a situation he was not familiar with. So, the forest supervisor—stepping past the district ranger—assigned me to prepare the EA. Even though I had written timber sale EAs and laid out timber sales in the past, timber management and silviculture were not my responsibility or expertise. I was the Resource Officer in charge of range, wildlife, recreation, and other non-timber resources.

Taking the bull by the horns, I formed a forest-wide interdisciplinary (ID) team and we had our first meeting on Boulder Top. I explained that I was tasked with preparing an EA for large timber sales on the Top. To a person, including the forest silviculturist, everyone agreed we should pick either a no-action alternative or a few very-small-harvests alternative. No one wanted a good road to access the Top. Besides being uneconomical, the team felt it wasn't yet time to harvest any of the Top's timber; it was much more valuable for recreational and scenic purposes. This wasn't wilderness, but it was a unique ecosystem.

Part of the Supervisor's argument was that another insect epidemic could hit at any time, so let's cut the trees now and get a new forest started. Besides, we needed to meet the cut. My counterargument was that 'any time' could still be years if not decades off; and if it did happen, we would slowly harvest the standing dead just as had been done for years. That would help the local economy as it had for years, giving work to locals rather than timber corporations from out of the area. The ID team reasoned that a forest of standing dead would probably be visually preferable to a landscape of stumps, engineered roads, and more people driving those roads.

The work on this project was overshadowed by an even higher priority in my workload: finishing the new management plan for grazing cattle on the huge East Slope Allotment, which included portions of Boulder Top. The old plan allowed too many cattle for too long a season. The Forest Supervisor had told me two years earlier that he expected me to reduce stocking to eliminate the problem. If I did that, he said he would transfer me anywhere I wanted to go, since I would be very unpopular with local ranchers. Now I was wondering: would I get the transfer, but in disgrace if I didn't recommend a big timber sale to get the forest out of its timber sale bind? It was becoming obvious that the Forest would have a hard time putting up enough timber to meet its sales target. This would impact the supervisor's report card with his boss. Initially, I figured that wasn't my problem, but actually, I realized it might be.

The ID team was in full agreement, but I was the one with the final responsibility for preparing the EA with its recommendation. How did the standoff turn out? The ID team met several times and we proceeded with developing our strategy.

All this took place over three decades ago. I honestly don't remember how it ended, but I did get my own transfer off the district before either the EA or the grazing plan was completed. After I left, I really didn't care anymore and I haven't been back since.[4] That is too bad because Boulder Top is a special place, and I hope that magnificent forested plateau is still picture-perfect, with tall spruce trees mixed with flower-studded meadows. And if those spruce are a standing ghost forest, there will be a new generation of trees growing up among the ghosts.

---

4 Slipped among this group of essays, I found a faded newspaper article from a Utah newspaper dated several years after Jake left the forest. The management plan for the forest was changed by a Forest Plan amendment converting the management for Boulder Top from timber emphasis to semi-primitive recreation emphasis. This meant no large timber sales were made and would not be made on Boulder Top. I don't know why Jake didn't include this information in his *Ghost Forest* essay. I suspect he was done with it, and that he must have smiled to read that his efforts eventually paid off.

Part II Photo Gallery

Fig. 11: "...many thought the entire area belonged in national park status." (p. 56)

Fig. 12: "...she continued a long tradition of family hiking dogs." (p. 61)

Fig. 13: "...silence reins over a landscape etched with draws and gullies and canyons building in intensity...." (p. 65)

Fig. 14: "Each time you stumble through the spruce forest to reach the edge of the plateau top, you will draw in your breath in a sudden gasp...." (p. 72)

Fig. 15: "It was peaceful up on the Point and I wanted to enjoy it for a while longer." (p. 73)

Fig. 16: "…graze their livestock in the summer months on the mountain or range lands that remained in federal ownership." (p. 78)

Fig. 17: "...the highest-elevation forested plateau in North America." (p. 83)

Fig. 18: "...the new forest was a healthy, young, almost-mature forest among the standing dead skeletons." (p. 83)

Part III

A Time and Place

Jake's Introduction

Time—the deep time of geologic history—is one of my favorite subjects. Since living and working in the Utah slickrock country three decades ago, I have become enamored, entranced, and enchanted by the whole concept of geology and its relevance to time. The very minuscule time of human history—much less my own even more microscopic segment of that—pales when seen from the deep time aspect of our Earth.

Place is an aspect of time since we become fixed in a specific geologic, biologic, and social location. Philosophers talk about a sense of place, a location where we feel comfortable, where we belong, and where we live, or at least visit.

After a life of moving to new places, discovering new ecosystems, new friendships, and new jobs, I became fixed in time and place in what I now consider home in western Colorado. Over twenty-five years ago, Rachel and I moved here on the edge of Rocky Mesa, overlooking the North Fork Gunnison River valley, and have owned the property for more than three decades. It feels right and we have spent nearly all our time here seeing life from different perspectives in one place. It is home and home is the definition of a time and place that fits our very souls like a hand in a glove.

We have learned that even though we 'own' our forty acres—the trees, rocks, and our ability to do what we want—we in no way truly own the land (fig. 19). It and the junipers and phlox, the deer and owls and nuthatches, own us and we are visitors here with their permission. We have the responsibility to treat all of it with respect and to fit in without being intrusive. We have come to know every square foot intimately. This is different from an earlier life exploring and discovering a wide variety of places, but from a less intimate perspective: northern Idaho's lakes; Mt. Rainier National Park's forests and wildflowers; Colorado's Rockies; the Sierra's foothills; Utah's high plateaus; South Dakota's Black Hills; and many places in-between. I loved the explorations and discoveries, but I was always a visitor.

Even though I stopped my widespread roaming and discovering, I am still learning as I put all that information to a higher objective. As another saying goes, "the more you learn, the more you do not know." Amen to that. As I learn more about this small piece of western Colorado, the more confused I get. The history of the rocks and landscape of this place gets more garbled and complex than I ever imagined. To add confusion, the plants and the animals do not always act as textbooks say they should.

Our forty acres are in a rural setting, and we enjoy the diversity of nearby agricultural fields and orchards. Our own juniper forest is mixed with sage flats and riparian areas of willow, sedges and rushes, watercress, and cattails, not only in the streams but scattered across entire spring-covered hillsides. The two year-round spring-fed streams deeply cut in two drainages that slope down from the almost flat mesa onto the also gently sloping mesa below us, which is cut by the North Fork Gunnison River, with the Black Canyon uplift beyond. The expansive views are broad: the West Elk Mountains, Grand Mesa, the Uncompahgre Plateau, the distant San Juan Mountains, and the even more distant Ruby Range of Colorado's Rockies. All that is quite a mouthful and it is an eyeful as well. We are perched like eagles overlooking many geological wonders.

As a wildlife biologist, I appreciate the diversity. Our drainages are accessed only by foot; everything is covered by jumbled basalt boulders from the adjacent higher mesas. Geologists say the entire mesa—of which we are on the southern end—was a massive landslide that occurred something like 600,000 years ago; or, more likely, it is an accumulation of several landslides over thousands of years, probably aided by Grand Mesa's glacial meltwater.

This place has developed a sacred meaning to us and we treat it as a wildlife sanctuary. We muse about wildlife coming here to die: deer (nearly every year), a mountain lion, Great-horned owls. Death is natural and we consider it an integral part of life itself.

One reason we stopped the wide-spread wandering and exploring is that we have all we need within these forty acres. The ancient junipers—twisting and half-dead—are artistry in nature, as are the patterns and colors of the lichen-covered boulders. Add in the streams, the wet hillsides, the dry, sun-baked ridgetops, and the sumac-cattail tangles—it adds up to a paradise.

I have written about many other areas I have visited or lived in, but

I need to tell more about the intimate relationship within my own backyard. It is indeed about time and place. Here, time is the complex geologic history and its mind-numbing period going back hundreds of millions of years—too complex to summarize, but suffice it to say, we live on an ancient landscape—modified beyond recognition many times over many millions of years.

One can spend hours and days and years learning, discovering, and adding immense amounts of knowledge. But if one does not then do something with that information, it is all without deep meaning. I believe in the dictum that if you are not exploring, you are not discovering. And if you are not discovering, you are not learning, thus you are not growing, and if you are not growing, you are dying.

Being able to walk my trails throughout these acres any time I want—by stepping out the back door, slogging through fresh snow, enduring the baking heat of a June afternoon, or watching a thunderstorm light up the sky on an August night—we are blessed beyond anything I ever imagined or believe I deserve. Because of this privilege, I feel the need to share thoughts as I live my day-to-day life. If, in sharing these feelings, you can relate to some of your own special places in time, I have succeeded.

I Know You're Out There Somewhere

ALL THE HOURS I have spent wandering my trails—the hillsides, ridge-tops, and streams—I have come to know the land and the inhabitants. This is an ancient land, full of hidden history. On occasion, I have felt a presence watching me. Sometimes it is a group of deer, standing still on the hillside above me, blending in with the trees and rocks (fig. 20). Many times, a Great-horned owl has suddenly flown silently from a juniper as I walked within arms' reach. Birds are always twittering and calling from the sky and trees above and around me. I have come to expect them all. And, there are the times I feel the energy of a cougar/puma/lion silently watching me as I explore the daily mysteries and she explored hers, evading me and leaving no sign of her presence.

When I sit under a centuries-old juniper, I feel the energy as the sap flows in its journey from soil to needle tip. The wet hillsides of orchid, willow, rush, and mint nestle up against the sage and juniper-dotted semi-desert ridgetops. I listen for their story as they tell of changes in water flow over the decades and centuries.

But the sounds I really listen for are the unseen voices of spirits and ethereal energies of past peoples. I know people have lived nearby for millennia. For at least five hundred generations, humans have roamed the valleys, rivers, and ridges. When visiting the nearby Eagle Rock Archeologic Site for the first time, I felt the presence of spirits who floated over their former home. The air is full of the energy of the people who once lived there. I believe they visited 'my' hillsides and ridgetops in their human lifetimes. They did not travel here to enjoy the view but rather used this mesa to scope out the land below.

I feel the special energy that has clung to the rocks and ancient junipers for centuries. I know I can talk to them but do they hear? I want to listen to what they say. I can almost hear their humming and singing as the wind caresses the treetops. The birds talk to them, why can't I?

I know they are out there somewhere. What can they possibly say to me? Can they tell me about wooly mammoths that still hung out in the canyons? Do they hear the distant cry of the condor floating the thermals far above? Have they journeyed to the edges of the glaciers that hang off the edge of the peaks far above them? Can they hear the calls of the white-faced men now landing on the far-distant eastern and southern shores? Do they even know there are oceans many moons over the horizon?

Often, I sit on my ridgetop under a full moon and look over the valley below; the scattered lights of the farms dot the ghostly-white moon-shadows. When my silent friends once sat here, they saw no lights. The blackness below was darker than the blackness above. The stars were the same, and the air smelled fresher then. Their silence was as still as the silence I hear.

As closely as I look, as quietly as I listen, I cannot see or hear them. But I feel them. They silently watch me, wondering about me as I wonder about them. They are there as surely as I am here. What can I learn from them?

One late October afternoon as I sat in the warmth of another autumn day, awaiting the change of seasons, I realized what this silence meant. Someone once long ago sat here just like me—possibly on the lichen-covered boulder—looking at the same mountain ridge on the southern horizon. He didn't see the same things though; his was a pristine world compared to mine, simpler, purer. He was asking the same questions as I was. Who was out there? He felt the presence of higher beings, spirits who knew all the answers to questions he was asking. What was it all about? Was there a god? He called his god by different names—Man Above, the Great Spirit, White Buffalo Calf Woman, White Shell Woman, Wakan Tanka. Lots of names for the same creator, the same guardian whom all paid homage to, prayed to, and asked for guidance and protection. It seems humans have searched for this ever since we fell out of the trees on the African savanna and started asking questions. That seems to be what sets us apart from every other being. We have been asking questions of our creator ever since we invented that creator and set him or her apart. Why should my quest be any different?

I feel someone out there. It isn't just ancient ancestors who roamed this area many millennia ago. It is the same spirit the ancestors looked for. I do have something in common with the ancients. Someday I will find you. I know you are out there somewhere.

Bright Eyes

This land I hike during or after nearly every sunrise surprises me every time I lift my eyes above the boulder-covered slopes (fig. 21). It is diverse and varied, dry and wet, forested and open; it is full of life. And when I try to contemplate that life, it is difficult to find the words or even the thoughts to create a description.

It always comes back to the central question—what is life? I see life not only in the leaves of the sumac and juniper, not only in the raucous calls of the scrub jays and ravens, not only in the flicking tail of the doe and her spotted fawn, but also in the scaly flakes of the multi-colored lichens, even in the rocks themselves. Life flies toward the clouds, crawls through and under thickets of twigs and leaves, and hops toward me. Life is displayed in the white- and yellow-centered Sego lily, the brilliant velvet green of rain-soaked moss, the subtle blue of the mountain bluebird, and the reds of sumac berries. It is displayed in the ragged brown bark and weathered branches of the centuries-old junipers; and in the thorny new growth of wild roses along the streams.

I smile as I see a new life that has just emerged. What do those bright eyes of the day-old fawn see (fig. 22)? Instinct has spoken unheard directions for the fawn to lie flat on the ground while mother grazes nearby. Nearly stepping on the white-spotted brown fur, I look into the innocent liquid brown eyes seeing her world for the first time. What does she think? This thing called life has created another miracle. But where did it come from?

Walking off-trail, I encounter a brand new flock of young turkeys, a dozen just emerging from eggs lying broken in a jumble. Mother hen wanders around clucking, nudging these stumbling new lives. Their eyes search for the first time, seeing me as another strange object. They follow Mom as she calmly leads them away, soon lost in tall grass.

Cottontail young lie in the nest until their bright eyes develop along with new legs and muscles. Soon the young hop quickly behind Mom, darting with bounding and erratic speed I cannot follow.

It is easier to watch the slow, almost unmoving life of cattail and watercress in the streams, cactus growing out of cracks in boulders, and ancient lichens covering dead juniper branches.

I wander from ridge-top to stream-bottom, rocky-hillside to rose-thicket. Life surrounds me in so many forms. It is all a miracle. Life arises, lives, grows, then dies—sometimes peacefully, sometimes violently. Then it arises again in never-ending continuity. It has been here longer than the rocks, the clouds, the blue sky. Did it arise in that deep blue-black vacuum that stretches in all directions to infinity? Was it created by some force we humans have been searching for as long as we've asked questions?

We have a consciousness that seeks answers. Do other forms of life apart from us think? When I look into those large fawn eyes, I cannot but think she wonders about me. She may not ask where she came from, but does she think about what she will do next? How can a plant think about anything? I see the sunflower turn its bright yellow blossom as it follows the sun from sunrise to sunset; does that not indicate some consciousness?

I watch with curiosity as the bull snake slithers out of sight behind a pile of rocks. Does he ever wonder what it would be like to run on two or four legs? I look overhead to see ravens chase a golden eagle. Is he as frustrated as I am when I am tormented by the gnat or mosquito?

People more perceptive than me have stated that nature is amoral. There is no good or bad in nature—life just happens. I cannot believe the eagle is bad if he swoops out of the sky and grabs a cottontail, ripping it to bloody shreds to feed his young. The thistle is not bad, although I uproot and spray as many as I see since it came in uninvited and will take over a field or hillside. It is displaying its success at reproducing and isn't that what life is about? Can there be a good aspect of a tick or mosquito? No, there doesn't need to be. Everything is here, connected in an intricate web of life, displaying complexity that is beyond understanding. Things are the way they are. But still, one wonders if there may be some overriding meaning, some universal consciousness that connects not only all life on Earth but all life in the universe.

What would it be like to ride high on a July afternoon thermal as it swirls invisibly upward in advance of an approaching thunderstorm? If I could only have those eagle eyes for a few brief moments, would my perception of all life below me change? My resident eagle often sits on a power pole next to a neighboring prairie dog field, watching for an inattentive rodent who can be his next meal. The little dog watches intently from his burrow, barking his annoyance at all who might wish to do him harm. But enough get careless to feed the eagle. Enough do not as they repopulate the field. The give and take happens every day and every night. Many more eyes than mine are on constant alert.

Life comes in many forms, so many that I am sure I would count into the thousands before listing what I could find on my little piece of diverse land. But that still begs the underlying question: what is life? I am constantly questioning the amount of time displayed in the rocks and mountains that surround me. Life of some form has been here before—since the deep time I obsess about. I can question the meaning of deep time. How about deep life? Life cannot stop at the edge of our atmosphere. What kind of life exists out there in the stars and galaxies that dot the night sky with diamonds and spirals of light?

When the deer fawn's eyes open for the first time, are they seeing something new, or just a continuation of something else? I cannot go back and witness the formation of the Wingate sandstone or the San Juan volcanoes; I will never know where life came from or where it will evolve far into the deep future. Maybe someday, some eyes will open for the first time and I will see something new for me. Will I remember all I learned before then?

Land of Deep Time

I have commented previously that I know the name of every former owner of Ravens Nest. There have been only five, including me. Five have had a piece of paper claim we each owned the land. Of course, that goes back less than one hundred years.

I have also stated that I do not own the land; it owns me. I only need to sit on a rock on any of the three ridge tops to understand this. As I walk out to the fence line delineating that someone else downhill from me is owned by their land, I walk on the rubble from a long-ago landslide. Very long ago according to the geologists—as in over half-a-million years. Possibly during a glaciation event, when melting ice and a once-in-a-thousand-year-rain or -snow deluge; possibly sparked by an earthquake as the weight of the ice pressured deep down movement of the Earth. A huge slab of the eastern end of Grand Mesa slid and moved with the speed of a jet airplane—thundering and rolling boulders and mud—thousands of acres of the displaced mountain that eventually would be my mesa.

No human was present to see or hear this. Some animals are still buried under dozens of feet of this mud, gravel, and rock. Some trumpets, screams, and bleats still echo underneath all this turmoil. I always listen for it but have never heard it.

But that is only a recent event. The boulders now dotting the hillsides (and the buried rocks that frustrate me as I try to dig post holes), are the black and lichen-covered remains of numerous lava flows (fig. 23) up on that mountain. Earth some twenty million years ago—before any hominids existed—was belching forth lava, ash, steam, and rock fragments that had slept deep underground. The West Elk Mountains and the San Juan Mountains were being formed—maybe at the same time lava flowed over the uplifted sediments that are part of the Colorado Plateau, on top of what is now Grand Mesa. Those rocks were a valley bottom surrounded by higher cliffs of the most recent sandstones. The lava created a vast lake that filled the valley; the surrounding softer rocks eroded over a vast period of time and left the hardened lake to be the modern top of Grand Mesa. And for millennia, my land has received tumbled boulders peeled off the edge of that ancient lava lake.

All this is still evident. I look behind me to see the basalt cliffs thousands of feet above me on Grand Mesa. Then I look east and south and see the peaks of the West Elk Mountains, and the more distant San Juan Mountains, with the pyramid top of Uncompahgre Peak lifting higher than anything else nearby. Smoke and fire filled the sky for millions of years as the earth trembled while it rose and changed.

On the south end of our central ridge, the landslide rubble is thin and the underlying sedimentary rock lies exposed. All the landslide slid on top of something and that something sits hidden below me, but not hidden all across the valleys of the North Fork, Gunnison, and even the Colorado River. Below, it is called the 'dobies or the badlands. It means that around 90 million years ago, I would be drowning under the great inland Cretaceous Seaway that stretched for hundreds of miles in any direction. I can reach down and touch the rock that once was mud carried from as far as the Appalachian Mountains, a continent away.

If I wanted to dig further—which I don't need to do since I can drive a few miles to the west and see the remnants of what lies below my land—I can see the history displayed in rock after rock for the past billion years. It is the sedimentary wonder called the Colorado Plateau and it extends below me for thousands of feet: in depth and in time.

Below that, my mental wandering through time ends with the granite and gneiss basement rocks, which are easily seen less than twenty miles south, just behind Green Ridge that blocks my view of the Black Canyon of the Gunnison. That is over a billion years old, and below that basement, I go no further. It is beyond my comprehension, but if I wanted, I could sit on my ridgetop until midnight—when I could continue for many billions of years as I looked at distant galaxies that existed and exploded before our galaxy was even formed from stardust.

Of course, by this time, I want to go back and study the piece of paper claiming I own this land. Do I own the time that existed before that paper was created? Do I own that Cretaceous sea or the sandstones that came from mountains that I will never see, eroded into nothing so long ago in deep time?

No one owns deep time; nor does anyone understand it. We see the evidence and marvel that it is pretty scenery. We think it is permanent, as solid as the Earth. Well, I am standing on and looking at evidence that the Earth is not very solid nor is it permanent. I am like a grain of sand in the vast expanse of sandstone lying thousands of feet below me.

I do marvel at the view, but I have to head back to my house, built on top of all that rubbly shale and sandstone. And I try not to think about what I 'own'. No one owns time and no one owns the land. As for trees and chipmunks and lichens on the black boulders? Well, that is another subject for another day.

Owls and Nests at Ravens Nest

I STOOD LOOKING AT the owl barely fifteen feet away from me. He was upright and rigid on a pile of dead asters next to the pond, wing feathers jack-strawed out, but the wings tucked where they should be. He barely blinked as I quietly talked to him. I told him he would be okay. He seemed stunned and not fully aware of me or anything else. I hoped he had only knocked himself silly chasing a mouse; he was too magnificent to soon be leaving this earth.

We've lived with Great-horned owls for the thirty-odd years we have been at Ravens Nest. The owls are part of this place, a symbol of the wildness and freedom we feel here; they have nested here for most of these decades. We call one of the irrigation ponds the Owl Pond, which is located above the Owl Tree, and there is an Owl Trail. In January and February, pairs sit on top of our house and on the nearby power poles.

As I talked to the seemingly injured owl, I thought back to when I met my first Great-horned owl. It was the summer of 1967 at Uncle Chuck's and Aunt Mabel's mountain cabin west of Boulder. My dad, brother, and I went up to the cabin, where cousin Jerry angrily shooed a Great-horned owl off the porch. I was amazed at the size of the bird. Jerry said it was hanging out on the porch, making a mess where it sat all day.

After that, I rarely saw an owl, until we bought Ravens Nest and camped in the old cabin on the west side. The cabin was full of mice and accumulated filth from years of neglect, but we cleaned it out and camped in it during our short visits those first years. The first spring, we noticed a pair of young owl heads peeking out from the top branches of a nearby juniper. We didn't see a nest but knew it was near. The next winter, while walking on the trail below the pond, we saw something odd sticking out from a massive nest in a centuries-old juniper. I helped Rachel up so she could grab the object, but as she reached for it, a huge bird flew out (fig. 24). I shouted, "look out!" and Rachel ducked and covered against the trunk. It was a Great-horned owl on the nest. Now we knew where one of the perennial nests was located, so rerouted the trail. This became the Owl Tree, and for years we kept track of owls and nestlings. I was surprised that owls bred and nested in mid-winter, but to fledge by May, the young birds require several months to reach their tremendous size.

Six years later, two weeks after moving into our new home, we were serenaded at 6 a.m. that first February by a Great-horned owl on the roof directly over the bedroom. When I opened the sliding door to look up on the roof, the owl leaned over the edge to look down at me a few feet below. We both did a double take. He obviously enjoyed sitting on the highest point around to call for his lady—two types of calls, his distinct four-hoots, and hers a mewl-like answer.

Most years, we would not hear them for months, then occasionally hear one in the distance. When a neighbor one year mentioned owls living in her barn, I accused her of stealing my owls. Some years, we would not see or hear an owl, guessing they needed a year or two of wandering. Or maybe new owls came into the territory abandoned by our old friends. Often while hiking Ravens Nest trails, we disturb one sleeping in a tree and it silently flies off. They make no sound when they fly; research tells why: their wings are shaped to allow wind to silently glide by a feathered edge that is uncommon in most birds. On one hike, our border collie scared an owl sitting on a very low branch; flustered by the indignity of a measly dog disturbing its morning snooze, it left a white calling card on her nose and she chased it all the more vigorously.

We always monitored the Owl Tree, watching the family from a respectful distance. One April, the nesting was very late, but momma was on the nest. Then, approaching carefully one day, I saw something that bothered me, something below the nest. Moving closer, I could only gasp in horror. Momma was hanging from a branch by one claw; blood dripped off her beak and spotted the ground. The owl was dead. I saw no evidence of the cause of death. I went back to the house, got Rachel and she carefully climbed up and through the ancient branches, to find two dead chicks next to a partial rabbit carcass; they had starved to death with no one to feed them. The timing was significant, since the next day, April 21, hummingbirds arrived right on schedule. Three lives of a very large and powerful bird gone, but the tiniest of birds coming back for the season to start new lives. Life does go on, with nature giving and taking as it always has.[5]

---

5   The full essay about this sad event, *Tragedy at the Owl Tree*, is included in the book "Zephyr of Time."

So—coming back to the present, I wondered if the owl now sitting un-moving staring at me was to join the procession of life. What had happened?

One of our tenants had called earlier on her cell phone to tell me about an owl she was looking at during her hike. Her dogs had not disturbed it and she thought it might have a broken wing. What to do? I told her to leave it; it was probably knocked silly and would soon recover. I waited about fifteen minutes, then went down to the pond myself. Yes, the owl was still there, where I watched it for a few minutes, hoping it would recover. Had it just stunned itself?

This reminded me of songbirds that have flown into our house windows. Most of the time, they bounce off and fly away. Once in a while, one really crashes and falls to the deck, sitting there for several minutes not moving; they gradually come to, stand up, and fly away. Rarely, do they hit so hard that they break their necks. In those instances, I carefully pick up the body and lay it on the shed roof so birds-of-prey or small meat-eaters can have a meal.

But would this owl join that sad group of birds or would it revive and fly off? I came back up the hill to let our other tenant know. A very spiritual person who was comfortable talking to animals and spirits, I figured she might be able to communicate with the owl. I know that might sound odd, but I felt she might be able to help the owl by methods I didn't have.

Angie appreciated the notice and she hiked down to the pond. After an hour, I thought I would go down and see if the owl was still there. As I approached the pond, I saw Angie sitting cross-legged on the ground about twenty feet away from the bird. She was in obvious meditation so I quietly turned around and left. The next morning I hiked back down to the pond and the owl was gone. Later, Angie said she was being taught by the owl, it was not injured but sent to teach her.

I would have let this be the end of a strange episode, but several weeks later, I found a dead owl on the near side of the pond, about fifty feet away from where I had seen the owl earlier. Lying in a tangle of cattails and watercress, it had died after all, although it had flown across the small pond. Maybe it had hit a tree or ground so hard, it caused fatal injuries. Or maybe it really was a spirit who came to teach Angie and departed this world after achieving its mission. One can believe what one wants. As a biologist, I am inclined to believe the former. As someone who is open to spiritual worlds, I am still tempted to believe the latter.

Radical Nature

I HAD TO GO down to Laughingwater Creek to think about the latest book I was reading. It is called "Radical Nature." Its premise is that not only do humans have a soul and consciousness, but all of nature does. Not just the plants and animals, but the very atoms, the protons and electrons, and even the quarks that make up everything. The entire cosmos is alive, with purpose and meaning.

I needed to think about the whole concept. I already believed that all plants and animals are connected by a complicated web of life, but the entire universe alive? That was a rather tough concept to swallow.

The creek is my go-to place to think about difficult subjects. I can sit in solitude, along the burbling creek, the birds calling hidden in thickets, and the breeze in the trees. It was early November so the crickets and buzzy insects were silent. The cattail angels were almost ready to float and fly in the changing winds of autumn, still a week or two away from full explosion. The reds and oranges and yellows of autumn had faded as the leaves now carpeted the ground, awaiting the sleep of winter. The two light snows early in the week still dotted the shaded areas with white (fig. 25), but most had melted.

Do the atoms of oxygen in the snow and water have a consciousness? Have they been part of the soul of the universe since the very beginning? Did the Big Bang know what it was doing? Is the very heart of an oxygen atom connected to all other oxygen protons and electrons? Does the universe have a meaning and some hidden purpose?

The very thought of all this stretched my imagination with incredulity, but I like to think I am open-minded. To me, it is very obvious we know very little about life and the universe, especially how everything is inter-connected. It was John Muir who said that everything is connected to everything else in the universe. In his colorful language, he said "hitched" rather than connected. It meant the same. Was he on to something? I looked up Muir's quotes and found another gem: "Every hidden cell is throbbing with music and life, every fiber thrilling like harp strings." Muir was as connected with nature as no one has ever been. Maybe all his cells had souls and had them since creation. But everything else?

When I look into the brown eyes of a doe with a fawn, I sense a consciousness that burrows into my heart. Is my soul connected to the eagle, the sandstone cliffs, the rain that falls in a July thunderstorm?

The thought of this will surely challenge all of us to rethink not only what life is about, but what the entire universe is about. That last subject goes way beyond my ability to even consider.

We cannot understand the immensity of both space and time. Maybe the individual atoms of my brain cells are alert and conscious, but the signals they send to my body? There is a disconnect somewhere in there.

I wonder if the buck hears some signal from the plants he eats that says, "Come here and let me nourish your body. My calcium wants to help grow your bones." I do remember from my college days how research shows a deer or elk knows which twig to eat from a plant. They eat the leaves and twigs with higher nutritional content. How can they know? How does the beaver know which tree to fall and how to lay the dam? I hear the word instinct used a lot, but what is instinct? How do you explain the fact that a person knows not to walk down the trail just before the rock or tree falls onto the trail? Some sixth sense? Well, what is that sixth sense? Is there a seventh and an eighth sense? Is there consciousness floating throughout space that knows things that can only communicate with our brain atoms and protons?

All I can say is, "I don't know." I think this whole subject is beyond our ever knowing. I know some folks will say with confidence that what I am talking about is God. A creator God who is within us and everything else. I also know some still see a conflict between science and faith. The two might be compatible and then again they might not. I cannot say. We all have our own beliefs and no one can prove us right or wrong. I am confident we will never be able to prove either case.

So why do I try to understand something that is beyond human understanding? I ask the cattail but get no answer. I ask the dragonfly, but she just flies away at supersonic dragonfly speed. The water continues to flow downhill, carrying oxygen and hydrogen atoms that have been floating around the universe for billions of years. If they have a consciousness, it cannot at this time connect with my consciousness. Or can it? And does it? I get this strange feeling. Call it instinct?

From Quarks to Ice

From the earliest moment of creation, the quark was dominant. Quarks—a made-up name for things that make up everything else in the universe—ruled the hotter-than-hell baby universe. As everything cooled, quarks settled down to form protons and neutrons and electrons, which then coalesced to form hydrogen and helium atoms. Then—after stars formed and died—gold and iron and all the other elements of the periodic table were created. We are made of quarks, as well as atoms of hydrogen and oxygen and carbon, which then make up bone and blood and water.

The lower hillsides of Laughingwater Creek are covered in springs. We do not have two or five or ten separate springs, but entire hillsides that seep. We call these hillsides 'wilderness' and my one attempt at creating access is named the Wetfoot Trail. Cattail thickets, rare bog orchids, wild roses, dogbane, sedges and rushes, and thistles cover the slopes. Basalt boulders—VW-size, sitting-in-the-sun-size, and tripping-over-size—are the hillsides' foundation, as they are everywhere else at Ravens Nest. Here, the boulders are hidden by the wildness that thrives in the year-round wetness.

Standing on the bank of Laughingwater Creek the day before the 2019 winter solstice, I saw quarks and atoms in their current forms: ancient, twisted junipers; brambling twenty-foot tall wild rose briars; sumac and cattail thickets; moss-covered boulders. Undulating, miniature glaciers snaked down the hillside (fig. 26) until they reached the still-flowing stream; ice, as water from the spring-covered slopes, 'flowed' downhill, obeying the other phenomenon that evolved from the earliest moment of creation: gravity.

The ice-artistry of the area does not, of course, exist in the summer, even though long-dead gnarly junipers dot the hillsides. It is in the frozen depths of winter that the seeps and rivulets of running water become sculpted ice flows. Often a foot or more thick, the slowly seeping water freezes into twisted and ropey forms creeping down the slopes.

During the rest of the year, the water winds and wends, hidden among the boulders and vegetation; its origins lie protected within the life above. In the depths of winter, there are no more secrets. The frozen flows build up into sculptures that only Mother Nature's quarks can create.

Sometimes the flow is rope-thin, snaking downhill. Others widen into massive growths engulfing everything below. They wind around and encompass the bases of the massive junipers and boulders, eventually reaching the flowing stream filled with dormant emerald-green watercress. Sometimes the ice masses stop as if deciding they proved their ability to fascinate—reminding me of an artist's tombstone epitaph in the Mendocino, California, cemetery: "An artwork is never finished, you just stop in a good place."

The streams seldom freeze, and often ice forms along the edges or where water has splashed from numerous small waterfalls (fig. 27). These edges and splashes create intricate sculptures among the cattails and other stream-side vegetation. In the winter of 2018-19, our lower Cabin Creek also froze, (due to the abnormally low water flow of an historic drought). Through the translucent ice, we could see trickling water. It brought back memories of the Conejos River in southern Colorado, near River Springs Ranger Station, my first Forest Service assignment in the early 1970s. That respectable river entirely froze over, as temperatures often hovered dozens of degrees below zero for weeks at a time.

With Ravens Nest's streams entirely spring-fed, the water temperatures are well above freezing. By the time the streams leave the property, the water has not had time to freeze, even on the coldest nights. However, the small flows, falls, and splashes freeze into ice sculptures as they quickly lose their heat. Whatever the reasons, the ice flows are enchanting as they snake their way downhill.

These seeping hillsides also remind me of the importance of water in our arid climate. To our north—in only a few miles and thousands of feet in elevation gain—wet meadows and spruce forests cover the landscape. That is the springs' source—pure Rocky Mountain spring water. The mountains squeeze water out of passing clouds and store it as snow. Come warm spring-time weather, the water is slowly released to feed the irrigation ditches of the dry lowlands; soaking through soil and boulders to a clay layer, to emerge on Ravens Nest's slopes. The hillsides are capped with dry juniper-sagebrush ridgetops. I can stand with one foot in the dry-site ecosystem, and one foot in the seeping-water ecosystem. Most of the water never reaches its natural destination—the Gulf of California and the Pacific Ocean. Humans' insatiable thirst for water to drink, to sprinkle lawns, and to grow alfalfa, changes its circulatory route through clouds and the atmosphere.

We can legitimately call it liquid gold since it is almost as valuable. An entire civilization west of the 100th meridian (located in the Great Plains), depends on this artificial and complex system. As I stand on the banks of my small stream and watch the ice inch toward the flowing water, I think of the importance of these frozen drops. To me, they are pure artistry, but a temporary phenomenon. They can freeze and melt and refreeze for a few months, but as the sun slowly returns north from its dark and frozen solstice, it inevitably releases the water drops to their eventual journey. Then I follow them, if only in my mind, as the cycle continues as it has for billions of years. And the quarks and protons and atoms are still there, reformed and re-arranged.

Standing along Laughingwater Creek—among the ancient junipers, the tangled sumac and roses, the moss and lichen-covered boulders, the sculpted ice, the clear cascading water flowing through the bobbing watercress—I imagine back eons when this land was new and I could see no evidence of people or civilization. We could have been standing here millions of years ago when quarks were, even then, ancient. The peace and quiet, as the stream flows by—as if time doesn't exist—are overpowering. I marvel at the atoms and quarks in the weathered life, in this ancient setting, surrounding us with proof of what a quark and an atom can do. And what we all can see if only we take the time to look.

Part III Photo Gallery

Fig. 19: "...we in no way truly own the land." (p. 95)

Fig. 20: "...deer, standing still on the hillside above me, blending in with the trees and rocks." (p. 98)

Fig. 21: "...nearly every sunrise surprises me every time I lift my eyes above the boulder-covered slopes." (p. 100)

Fig. 22: "What do those bright eyes of the day-old fawn see?" (p. 100)

Fig. 23: "...boulders now dotting the hillsides...are the black and lichen-covered remains of numerous lava flows...." (p. 103)

Fig. 24: "...so she could grab the object, but as she reached for it, a huge bird flew out." (p. 106)

Fig. 25: "The two light snows early in the week still dotted the shaded areas with white...." (p. 110)

Fig. 26: "Undulating, miniature glaciers snaked down the hillside...." (p. 112)

Fig. 27: "...ice forms along the edges or where water has splashed from numerous small waterfalls." (p.113)

Part IV

Tori's Songs

Bernice Sanderson's Introduction

After Tori died, I had the task of sorting through her papers. This was an exciting job although it was also painful for me since I understood the meanings behind her works. Many months after her passing, among Tori's files, I discovered more of Jake's writings. Nine of these comprise most of this Part.

Jake had written short essays and poems for Tori, with the intention of her using them, if appropriate, in her songs. He didn't think she would. But, after his passing, she used a few sentences and themes. For example, her songs *The Other Side of Eternity*, *Ancient Sentinels*, *Fire in the Sky*, and *I Know You're Out There*, are all based on his writings. At the time—honoring Jake's request for anonymity—she credited the lyrics to herself since many of the words were hers, but the ideas and lines in italics are Jake's.

In addition, there is one essay separate from the rest. This was written by Tori, not as a song, but as a personal remembrance, shortly before her passing, long after Jake's death. *The Visit* gave me chills when I first read it. Now, putting together this final manuscript—which includes Jake's *Spirit Man* and *Spirit Woman* (Part Six)—I get more than chills. It is frighteningly prescient.

The Visit[6]

By Tori Reynolds

I know my time is drawing to a close. I've lost my closest friends and family, and know I am growing more philosophical and withdrawn. I've led a wonderful life and have been part of this land I love more than anything. I remember my discussions with Jake as he was in the same position I am now. He was at peace and was ready to move on. I am as well.

Recently I've shared a lot of personal time with Bernice and had great discussions, trying to share my wisdom, such as I have, with her. I've also been putting final touches on a song that I hope summarizes my beliefs.

Today, I walked out to the point on the west ridge and sat on a rock. It was quiet this May morning, with hummingbirds buzzing past me, wildflowers blooming after a wet spring, and ravens circling overhead, calling to their new fledglings from the nest in the tall tree down by the creek below. Their squawking broke the quiet but I've grown used to it and find it part of the peaceful feeling of place and time.

During his last days with us, Jake seemed changed. I know he liked to sit in this spot and think, gazing past the valley below, to the distant snow-capped mountains. Maybe he had a vision or a revelation—I don't know since he didn't share his experiences with me. But today, I wanted to see if maybe I could tap into the understanding he gained. I half thought he probably met angels (fig. 28) or aliens or whoever he was communing with.

I closed my eyes and hummed several of my favorite songs. A few of them I had composed for him, incorporating thoughts and words he had secretly written for me. A strange 'electric' feeling in my head forced me to stop humming. I wondered if I was having a stroke. I closed my eyes and sat—fearfully still and silent.

I then heard what sounded like a rush of wind. I opened my eyes, but I could not clear them; it was as if a hazy film was covering my eyes.

---

6   Absent from Ravens Nest the day Tori experienced this and wrote about it, I returned two days later to find her on the floor—taken away by Al, Rachel, and Jake. I will always remember the peaceful look on her face. She had worked that previous evening finishing her final song. I cannot listen to it all these years later without weeping.

Then I heard a gentle laughter. I recognized it: Jake's voice. I thought I was hallucinating, but still had my other senses: I felt the rock I was sitting on and heard birds singing. Then I saw a small black dot that grew larger. The haze cleared from my eyes. The dot turned into a human figure as it came closer.

"Oh, my God," I said aloud. It was Jake and his voice became clearer.

"What a nice sight, Tori. I haven't seen you for a while."

I may have screamed, and nearly collapsed, but I'm not sure.

I stood up. Jake embraced me, but I could not feel anything. He laughed again and said we could not touch, but he felt my energy.

Again, all I could say was "Oh, my God,"

Jake laughed harder. "No, I am not God. Quit saying that."

"Are you real? No, of course not. You are dead."

"Tori, you are a bright person, full of imagination and creativity. Look at all your work, your lyrics, your music. Put that brilliance to work. Do I look dead and gone forever?"

"But, but..." I stuttered.

"Remember one of my favorite phrases? Think about it—Think this through.

"What are you experiencing right now? Is it a dream? Am I a figment of your imagination? You have a creative imagination. Is this not real? How can you tell? Was I part of your imagination? Or are you a part of my imagination? Or are we both part of a larger imagination of a much higher intelligence? Is Earth part of the imagination of such a powerful entity? You don't know, do you?"

"Jake, quit playing with my mind. You used to do things like this. You know I don't know the answers to those questions. Do you?"

I stared at this image of Jake. He stared back but with a slight smile.

"What do you think, Tori?"

"No, I refuse to play that game anymore. I want answers. You know them, don't you?"

Jake laughed as he put his hands up in the air. "Yes. And you will too, soon. Very soon. Tori, you and I had a special bond. I loved you like a daughter. Look at you now. You are a true elder. A fountain of wisdom. People look up to you. I am proud of you."

We talked for a few more minutes but then he became silent. We looked at each other, then I asked, "Are you here to take me away? I feel tired and old."

"I will welcome you but not right now. You are amazing and I am proud to have known you and been a special friend. Your time is close and I am looking forward to catching up. You are ready. Everything will be fine. I wish I could stay longer, but I must go. Goodbye for now."

With that, he held out his hand to touch me, but as he said, we could not connect. He started going backward, slowly fading into that small dot.

This was not a dream or a hallucination. What was it? I have no idea, but I know Jake will explain it to me. In his last days, he seemed so distant and in a way, so full of the wisdom of things I could not understand.

After this encounter, I am starting to understand. I know he wrote a lot of things I have not seen, and I know some of them will seem strange and incomprehensible. I will wait and let him explain them to me. I am now ready. The time indeed is near.

Journey With the Wind

Standing on the ridgetop, facing into the wind. April blowing by. Gusting over thirty mph. I watched ravens playing high above, soaring in the wind, turning, swirling up to dive again. I longed to join their journey.

But I had my own to think about. *The wind awakened memories of my long and erratic journey* to get to this place. Not only this location but this time of my life. A lot had changed. The winds were different, each type signaling different turns in my journey.

Soft breezes took me to peaceful moments on high peaks, lakeshores, grassy expanses of meadows and wildflowers. A herd of cow elk with their nursery of calves (fig. 29), miles from a trailhead in Colorado wilderness.

Sea breezes full of salt spray led me to lean over the tour boat railing *to see a humpback. Or to look in awe at a glacier calving ice into towering ocean splashes.*

Winter gales, blowing snow in blinding whiteouts along Wyoming, Nebraska, Colorado, and South Dakota highways. Facing blowing snow along a disappearing trail in Colorado, cross-country skiing back to my truck, parked along a highway disappearing under a blanket of moving snow.

Making myself comfortable on a lichen- and moss-covered boulder, I adjusted my goggles to protect my eyes from dust and pollen. I pondered what wind is. Of course, I know it's moving air. Simple molecules of oxygen, nitrogen, carbon, motes of dust from distant mountains or deserts. But what made it move?

I tried to see above the wind. Or maybe beyond it. How high did it go? Where did it start?

Watching clouds scutter by, torn by a gale higher in the atmosphere, I know the wind has been here forever. Since the earth settled down four billion years ago—with seas collecting their supply of water and volcanic eruptions adding new gases with rising heat—the air has been moving. From gentle breezes to howling gales, carrying dust, water, and snow. For millions of years, the wind collected living things: pollen and seeds, pterosaurs and pterodactyls, birds and bats, and butterflies.

The wind has been alive and searching forever. Poets and writers, musicians and physicists have written and sung and studied the wind as long as humans have tried to walk on two feet. No one has captured the essence of the wind. It is the ultimate symbol of freedom. Not only can we fail to adequately predict it, but we also cannot even describe it. We search for meaning and find mystery.

I tried to tie my journey to the wind but failed at that as well. My journey had shifting directions and speeds. For much of my life, I said my goal was attaining wisdom. It has been lack of wisdom that allowed me to make such a statement. Could I even describe what wisdom is? Wisdom is not a collection of facts, an encyclopedic knowledge of science, human behavior, and other things learned from books and from living a diverse life. It is not getting straight A's in school, or how many degrees you can earn. What is it and how would I know if I attained it?

Age is a necessary ingredient, but many older people are not wise. Attaining wisdom is like understanding the wind. *A journey is not achieving a destination or a specific goal. A journey is just that—an experience.* Experience and understanding are a product, and maybe that is wisdom. What experience does the wind have? The wind does not aim for a specific location. It moves, it changes, it creates consequences. But it does not learn.

A dried stem blew by. Dust swirled near my feet, carried by the wind but not the wind. Maybe my journey was not the wisdom I sought, but a product of my own mind. I was moving and creating consequences. Maybe that is wisdom after all.

Standing in the Wild

SLOWLY PICKING MY WAY down the rocky slope—stepping over lichen-covered basalt and sandstone boulders, prickly pear cactus, and fallen juniper snags—I mused about 'my' old-growth forest. Since there are few young trees, it has always been an art gallery of ancient, twisted, and gnarled giants. Not 'giant' in height—most are less than twenty feet tall—but in girth and heavy limbs. *I felt the long passing of time among the trees, the rocks, the far-off mountains, and the valley below.*

I sat beside one matriarch and rested my back against the trunk. I estimated the age as 400-500 years. Calling it a tree does not do it justice. It is a stately living work of art with more wisdom and history than I will ever have.

I thought about what it was, as well as what I was. It was not mobile and didn't look like animals, but it was alive. It has wood instead of bones; leaves instead of lungs that breathe in carbon dioxide and breathe out oxygen; an inner bark that carries food and water to all parts of the body via sap instead of blood. Its brain was somehow scattered throughout its body but I knew something coordinated all its living functions. It knew its place in this world in which it stood silent except for the quiet rhythmic melody of wind whistling through green needles and dead twigs. Half of the tree was bare of needles, long "dead" but still part of the body.

As I sat there, breathing in its exhalation of oxygen and giving it my carbon dioxide, I thought of my place in this world. *I explored many places, lived many adventures, learned many facts of life. But I still search for a meaning of place. I love this hillside, the rocks, the trees, the birds in the sky, the chipmunks and deer nibbling the greenery. I consider it a small wilderness. But do I belong in such a wilderness?*

I remembered wise words from Thoreau: "In wildness is preservation of the world." And Muir's advice to climb the mountains and get their good tidings. But here, Muir's words hit home, "I never saw a discontented tree. They grip the ground as though they liked it, and though fast rooted they travel about as far as we do."

I wanted to talk to this living being, but I didn't know its language. I wanted to ask what it had seen in its life. It was obviously here before

Europeans settled and started changing their world. It lived with the Ute, who may have sat at the base of this tree, too. But what would it have seen? Were there many tree neighbors? Did wolves and grizzlies roam the valley below? How far could it see, I wondered, as I squinted to see the distant mountains looming vaguely in the smoky haze of summer.

The world had changed around this ancient tree, but it continued to stand rooted in the rocky soil, its unmoving world not changing. Or did it? I loved the solitude I found here, but I was a visitor. I move around, constantly asking questions and looking for answers. Each answer creates a new question. Too much diversity? The tree reveled in its diversity, but it was limited. How many birds had sat on its branches, nested in its needles (fig. 30)? When it was young, deer may have nibbled on tender young branches. A coyote may have burrowed at its base. An owl could have nested high up in that large fork of a branch, now dead and bare.

Maybe the owl and coyote asked questions, too. Maybe coyote language resembles tree language. I did understand the language of the wind. It told me to stand firm, find my place, listen to the silence. It said to look for the relationships of all things and respect differences. We all need to live together. We will find our place. *We need the wild places, but they do not need us.*

As I stood to go, *I ran my hand over the rough bark remaining on the north side of the main trunk. I caressed the time-worn smoothness of the dead limbs. I think I heard a voice. Or maybe it was the wind. It said to find my place, then treat it and all around me with respect—wildness is in our minds and in the trees and mountains.*

Ancient Sentinels

THOUSANDS OF TREES COVER our sanctuary of ridges and draws. Nearly all are juniper, with a handful of pinyon scattered about (many showing scars of past porcupine encounters). We have researched which species of juniper grow here. Silviculturists' nomenclature has changed over the past century, and it appears DNA analysis is almost needed to distinguish Rocky Mountain juniper from Utah juniper. Whatever they are, they are natural sculptures. Many are ancient, 300 to 400 years old, or older.

The trees on the ridgetops and upper hillsides live in a dry setting. They are widely spaced, squat, and many-limbed (fig. 31). They show courage, stamina, and determination to survive in the tough environment. Go downhill to the creek—where water is abundant—and they look like 'real' trees, tall and crowded, competing with sumac and cattails. On the wet hillsides where springs saturate the ground, the junipers are ghostly, dead.

The wet areas show an interesting history: water increased and drowned the trees. They do better with some water, but not standing in water, as this ghost forest is. My guess is the irrigation of the last century in the fields above Ravens Nest has created an aquifer that flows out on my hillsides. Trees once flourished here like in other places, but the flood of water drowned them (fig. 32). Cattails, dogbane, rushes, and a rare bog orchid now carpet the feet of these skeletons.

Rachel has spent her spare hours over the years visiting every ancient juniper, assigning each a numerical name, photographing, drawing, and documenting their twisting and branching distinct forms, and their neighboring beings. They are unlike aspen or spruce forests, which blend one into another in endless processions up or down hillsides. I love them all, but junipers are the artists in the crowd—part of a diversity that enriches us all.

A common feature of these old sentinels is that they often are half-dead, with the apical meristem and entire branches bare skeletons (Rachel refers to this phenomenon as a unique-quality-of-deadness), but the remainder live with leaves and berries. The twisted, gnarled limbs reach to the sky. I wish they could talk. I imagine what they could relate to me as I ponder their past lives.

Sitting beneath one giant, I breath in and out, in unison with its own breath: it exhales oxygen while I inhale it; I exhale carbon dioxide, which the tree takes in. We share life. I try to see the energy, share its strength. I ask what this elder has seen in its life. I envision the scene it has viewed for these many centuries—wandering Utes, a few buffalo, mountain sheep, cougar, coyote, and rabbit. When it was a seedling, this was a land free of roads, towns, power lines, jet contrails. It has seen changes in the past 150 years that have altered its world, although the old sentinels have not moved an inch. It has grown and provided a home to owls, squirrels, and nuthatches; eagles soar overhead, deer winter under its warmth, and summer in its cool shade.

Why did two spiraling branches die? Have the berries sired new seedlings, such as the younger trees nearby (fig. 33)? Few are under five decades old. Will the old giant live another year or ten or one hundred? What will it be seeing four centuries from now? Will the view ever revert to what it was when the tree was a seedling? Where will the energy go when the entire tree is a leafless, lichen-covered statue, awaiting a spring wind that finally topples it?

We named the hillside between Spring Creek and Sage Flat the 'Old Forest'. Most junipers there are ancient, with very few youngsters. With an understory of four-wing saltbush, ricegrass and needlegrass—no cheatgrass or other introduced species—I assume this is what the area looked like when my ancient sentinels were young. I want to see the whole area like that. Can I go back in time when I close my eyes and breathe in the energy? Would I want to? Does nature show any preference? Do I show a bias when I think those past days were better? Better for whom or what? *As I sit under the old juniper, close my eyes, and ask the questions, I know I will not receive answers. But maybe I do. I feel the energy. It reinvigorates me when I breathe in the freshness and listen to the sound of the wind and the distant chickadee. When I look into the blueness of the sky,* I don't see the contrails. *I see only the eagle soaring high below the clouds.* Maybe I cannot go back 400 years or 4 million years. But if I only look at the tree or its neighbors, I see no other evidence of my kind. *I am alone with history. The history of the tree and its kind, not my kind.*

Fire in the Sky

THE CLEAR SKY WAS filling with high clouds, building fast. The cumulus were rising, billowing, darkening at the base, turning into massive forms as the pure white of their tops met the blue sky. As I've said, my favorite color is that edge of blue sky and white cloud (fig. 34); the contrast is blinding and magical.

The sky darkened as greys and blue-violets covered more of the sky-space. *I could hear far-off rumbles of thunder as flashes of lightning sparked among the cloud masses.* Soon, thunder echoed, bounced from peak to peak, ridge to valley, lasting seconds (or eons) until disappearing beyond the eastern horizon.

But I didn't look at the horizon. I didn't even look at the ground. *I was entranced by the sky.* Actually, I didn't want to see the ground at all. I didn't want to see the valley below or the mountain uplift to the south, the ridge of the long plateau to the west, or the jagged peaks to the east. They weren't there. *I was looking into the past, into deep time.* I have envisioned many times what happened in this very spot millions of years ago. I am obsessed with the geologic history of this very active spot on Earth. Massive changes have taken place over a billion years, but I wasn't interested in that—for now.

At that moment, I looked into the past in my imaginary, long-wished-for time travel. *That sky, those clouds, the lightning—they all had not changed in the billion years of time. As long as I look up to the sky, I see what has been going on for well over a billion years. The blue of the sky, the rolling in of the clouds, the formation of the thunderheads, the rising, billowing, changes in color—that was time travel. I could have stood here a thousand million years ago and looked up and seen the exact same scene above me.* Nothing has changed. Only when I lower my eyes will I notice changes. The uplift, then the total erosion of the Uncompahgre Range of the ancestral Rockies, the volcanoes of the San Juan and West Elk mountains, the great deserts that later formed the Wingate sandstone, the continent-wide Cretaceous Sea that would have put me a thousand feet underwater where I now stood, the endless river deltas and swamps that created seams of coal and colorful mud and sandstone formations I now can see stretched over millions of acres of the West—that all happened beneath this cloud-filled sky.

The chemical makeup of the sky has changed over time. Back then, there was more oxygen as the newly evolved green plants started freeing it up. Carbon dioxide was changing as volcanoes spewed ash and water into the sky, creating a haze that lasted for centuries. No jet contrails, nor black-feathered wings of ravens or pterodactyls. No life below. Just water droplets forming from the vapor of far-off seas. Seas that pounded coastlines; waves that rose and fell, evaporating the hydrogen and oxygen for its thousand-mile journey to endless cloud formations. There was no noise other than the wind whistling—not through treetops or grasses—but bouncing off rock cliffs and bare freshwater lakes and streams. The noise of water, either in the air or on the ground, water that created the energy that created heat that created thunderheads that created thunder. Lots of creation, but nothing yet that resembled life—at least on land.

Entranced, *the jagged, white-hot fire of the lightning bolts shot through my soul.* Cloud-to-cloud, jumping dozens of miles at a leap, dropping down to points of rock—dancing and zig-zagging another dozen miles in instantaneous trails of fire. They would start no fires since there was nothing yet to burn. Perhaps melt a rock cliff face, or melt a sand-dune to form a large slab of sandstone or molten slag.

Then, as I looked up and saw the past, it changed. The same lightning, the same downpour of rain, the same blast of wind—they all have consequences now. Trees burn, towns and fields flood, buildings blow down. Now, there is life. And me. Consequences may have changed, but the storms are the same. Time marches on, not knowing the difference.

The Other Side of Eternity

I OFTEN SIT UPSTAIRS looking at the view out my third-floor window. I've enjoyed this panorama—the distant San Juans, nearby Black Canyon uplift, the river and mesa in the valley below—every day for over two decades. I think I've finally come to understand the significance of the geologic history of this scene, stretching in time for over one billion years and countless upheavals of the very earth. I became part of the history, even when walking the trails down along my creeks, hidden from the macro view as I call it. On my streamside trails—in what I call 'down below'—I am surrounded by lichen-covered basalt boulders, springs that surface from the snow-meltwater of the high mesa to the north, and, the ancient junipers. I know that below my feet are shale and sandstone formations and other rock layers that stretch for miles below the surface and hundreds of millennia in the past. I feel surrounded by eternity—deep time and all its history.

I recently reviewed geologists' written histories of the Colorado Plateau. Since my exposure to deep time—while living in southern Utah—I have been entranced by the concept of the time now exposed in rocks hundreds of millions of years old. For a mind and body that will not last more than a century, this is a challenging task. I read that human minds cannot fathom the type of time span we are dealing with: *a hundred million years, or a billion. What is really the difference?* And, I am fascinated with the cosmos itself, which counts upward of fifteen billion years.

Let's just label these figures: eternity. They are beyond what is meaningful. *Is there something beyond the edge of the universe?* Is there another universe, or a parallel one, or several branes of multi-verses? *What is on the other side of eternity?*

Sitting on the southern edge of Ravens Nest's central ridge, I focus on where the Gunnison River flows out of the Gorge, which comes out of Black Canyon. This is a canyon I have yet to explore in detail. I think *we should all have mysteries we have yet to examine. To examine and discover the answers, or non-answers—to each mystery we encounter, we learn. And as long as we learn, whatever minute detail it may be, we can still grow and grab onto the secrets of life.* I want to know what is in that canyon. Although I doubt it will be anything new, it may be new to me. To be honest, almost everything that exists is new to me. *Does that mean I have to live forever in order to discover all I want to discover?* Or maybe I continue the discoverer's life on the other side of eternity, where the discoveries will dwarf everything.

But back to the Gunnison Gorge canyon. This is no small gap in the earth. Like so much in my view, this canyon would be noteworthy of some kind of formal designation anywhere else. It is the first view out my bedroom window every morning—unless hidden by rain or snow or fog. But even then, it is more special. Becoming jaded by such views is a challenge I try to avoid every day.

I have been accused of thinking too much. Life would be so much simpler if I just accept things that I see and hear. I have tried, without success. I envy those who can watch the world go by and be pleased by the joy of living. I am pleased by that joy but need to understand what makes it joyful.

A flock of ravens just passed by, headed across the valley towards the canyon. They seem bound for a determined objective, a place or thing that gives them meaning. Or maybe they are like me, searching for something they will never find. I wish them luck and a safe journey. Maybe I will meet them on the other side of eternity. Will we all find what we are looking for?

I need to lower my view and see the common things at my feet. I wander down to the creek, where the tumbling water flows between black boulders and watercress (fig. 35). That is something I can relate to. Algae and water plants live a life different than mine, but shorter. Of course, the boulders and the flowing water belong to the eternal existence beyond my understanding, but I ignored them for the moment.

All living things are like me. They have a finite life I can relate to. The frog will be eaten by the bull snake hidden in the willows. The willow will be eaten by the rabbit as he searches in the snow. The rabbit falls to the owl, who in a sudden thrust is devoured by the bobcat. The juniper is slowly killed, limb by limb by drought and beetles. So goes the unending circles of life and death. I prefer life, but know death is one half of the equation. I want to think that the rocks themselves have a similar life and death, but like the water, they are recycled, living forever. That eternity thing again.

Surviving the crisis that has been this year of 2020, I realize the tragedy of the pandemic will pass into history. Most of us will survive. The upheaval that was the election will pass. Future generations will ask what were they thinking back then. Things change, life goes on. *Life is change. Change is life.*

As I gaze into the distance, the San Juan Mountains are blurry on the horizon. The summer haze and heat make it hard to focus. That is appropriate since they represent a time millions of years ago when they were rather unfocused. Massive volcanoes, erupting and collapsing calderas, ash and cinders spewing skyward, all made this a rather forbidding and mystical landscape. Not now, though. I know that up there hugging the clouds is a magical expanse of land, glaciated, covered with streams of snowmelt and wildflowers, reminding me that life and land change. What once was, is now something different. *Eternity is a shifting concept and adapts to whatever we want it to be. I like the shapes and colors and forms. Once I become part of it, what will I look like?*

Kaleidoscope Sky

THE SKY IS SO easy to observe. You can stand and tilt your head back, although this can be uncomfortable if you look straight up. Sit in a chair or on a rock and you see the same thing. Turn your head and scan the horizon in all directions and you see the immensity of the sky. But lie down—on a grassy spot mingled with wildflowers or in a sandy clearing, feeling one with the earth—and you see into the blue infinity. When filled with clouds, it becomes an immense work of art.

Every day paints a new work. Even then, it changes as you look at it. You become an expert in clouds, and take that a step further and you observe the weather as it is being made (fig. 36).

I say all this from a viewpoint of the desert and mountain West. *The sky is a kaleidoscope of forms, and the hills and mountains constitute the painting's foreground. The sky extends as far as you want. The air is clear and a shade of blue that has no description. It is purity and serenity as only God can make it.* That is on a clear day.

When weather is being created, clouds can blur reality. Shades of grey and blue—outlined in billowing puffs or streaks of moving forms—grow and unleash your imagination, most often during monsoon season. In winter or spring, a front announces itself with a wall or diffusion of clouds, sky-high, and horizon-wide. Even then, the virga masses—rain that evaporates before reaching earth—can paint beautiful forms.

On a late spring day, watching clouds form and overtake the sky, the distant line of peaks of the San Juans faded and disappeared. I looked only at the clouds and traveled back in time. This could have been the very same sky that filled the view a million years ago. Or a billion. Time in the sky has not changed. Earth has: mountains have formed, eroded, formed again; rivers meandered, swamps filled and drained. But the sky stayed the same: water evaporated from nearby or distant seas; floated and drifted, maybe even raced across distances, then returned to Earth as rain or hail or snow; evaporated again and reformed clouds. As a child, I watched puffy clouds as they formed sheep or horses or birds. There was a time when clouds formed these same shapes but animals did not yet exist. What would I have thought then?

Now let's turn the sky dark as the sun lights the other side of Earth. The black sky is filled with stars and galaxies: you are looking into eternity. The vastness is not just distance, it is time. We are looking at the beginnings of everything—the beginning of time and the ingredients of life itself. The infinity of gases we call stars and galaxies is beyond our comprehension, but try to think of it anyway. Somewhere in that infinity is the spark that started it all. The plasma formed electrons and protons which then formed atoms that coalesced to form molecules that were moved by gravity. Each ball of gas that formed from this collection of molecules boiled and exploded to form elements. Then things got interesting, which eventually ended up being us. Now we look back and try to recreate what happened. I know it is easiest to look into the blackness and marvel that we are here and leave it at that.

The darkness of the night sky sparkling with light is so opposite to the daytime sky. All this is still out there, but our sight is limited to a blue background of a cloud-filled dome. Does this make it safer for us, easier to try to believe what we wish about life and gods and infinity?

My thoughts return to the present and to what I see now above me. But, I cannot resist looking only at the passing clouds, the collection of sheep and horsies and faces that I saw seventy years ago. I again begin the time travel that I love to do. I think back a million or even a billion years—as long as I do not look at the surface of this Earth—I am there. I stay there, floating with the clouds until I tire and need to return to the now of my life.

Zephyr

Two days of intense wind ended the month of September. Storms were brewing to our north and west, but we were left with blue skies, a few scudding clouds, and wind. A powerful *zephyr*. No dust, no haze. Just wind.

I walked the trails and stood by the pond as cattails swayed back and forth. No seeds yet to fly on the zephyr—they must wait a few more weeks. Good thing, I thought; they would have been shorn of the fluff that I look forward to on warm autumn afternoons. Colors had yet to mature, although I did see a few leaves of bright crimson on escaped Virginia creeper vines. Sumac was only starting to glow its yellow-orange (fig.37), hinting of days to come. But the wind was premature, in a futile attempt to strip trees and shrubs of leaves. It seemed everything this year was off-kilter. We had a very wet winter and spring that we thought ended a terrible drought. But summer returned to hot and dry. Time will tell, as life continues in cycles and circles, a theme I cannot get away from.

But the wind! What is this phenomenon? I know it is air: plain and simple molecules of oxygen and nitrogen, and the numerous other atoms that circle Earth and have been doing so for as long as Earth has been circling the sun.

I feel it is alive. Earth breathing heavily to rid itself of the poisons we humans have spewed into the atmosphere. That is another story that I do not wish to get into today, but this is indeed a spasm we should not ignore. How can anyone ignore this?

Standing on the ridgetop to catch the full effect of the zephyr, there is no dust, so I know that Utah is not blowing by. The wind seems clean and pure. Sometimes in the spring, we feel parts of China blowing by as the Gobi Desert seeks worldwide adventure. No, this is just wind that skirts a storm somewhere else. These are related to the winds fanning flames of California wildfires once again ravaging that state. I keep my fingers crossed that someone nearby does not light a match, and wish the zephyr would bring rain with it.

The wind carries in something else: it blows past the spirits I have often felt; it blows past the history of the land, changed beyond recognition from times long ago. *It blows my own history through, past, and out of me.* Into my eighth decade of existence, I have felt the wind flow past thousands of times. This fall, it awakened something in me that feels somehow different. I was not feeling the presence of others but of myself. I was feeling my history. My past experiences, thoughts, dreams, successes, failures, and desires all were teasing me with their presence. I wanted to grab onto them and go back. I knew I couldn't, at least yet. I thought of where I now stood, looking into a past with far more years than I had in my future. Was that me blowing by? My spirit? Is that something that exists, even if only on a passing zephyr?

I imagine there is some point where we all review our lives as we start the final journey. Maybe this was a preview: I heard the zephyr call to me as it blew past. The real zephyr is gentle, caressing, and soothing, like a lover, whispering kindness and happiness. This September zephyr is too powerful, yet it grabs onto my past as if it can't let go.

Are our spirits, our history, the lives we have lived and let go of, our memories, something real? Are they out there, awaiting the day we join them and move on to whatever is next? They may be out there awaiting the gentle zephyr breeze. I will bide this wild ride as the currents and shifting patterns of summer let go and prepare for a new autumn pastoral. *Circles and cycles I repeat to myself once again. Are our lives circles and cycles like the winds?* I will let this one blow past and settle down to the gentle breeze that will better reflect what I am searching for.

Deep Future

Three hen turkeys were parading up the Center Ridge Trail, clucking as if to tell me to get out of the way. Springtime. It means the arrival of wild turkeys as they mate and select nesting sites. We especially like to watch them fly up to the large elm tree to roost at night. Twenty-pound, fluttering turkeys are comical, shifting and rearranging themselves on thin branches thirty feet up.

Springtime is also when the apricot blossoms open well before the last mid-twenty-degree temperatures of winter. Most years, very few apricots make it to fruition, literally. Depending on springtime moisture, we always await the phlox, cacti blooms, Townsendia, and Sego lilies. This is semi-desert and not abundant with wildflowers, but we appreciate what we do get.

As I sat this year, after a winter of deep moisture and seemingly endless snow and cold, I was waiting for April showers that would guarantee flowers. Someone turned off the water tap and the deep winter moisture was slowly drying up. As usual, we needed rain.

But I was thinking of the present, a fluctuating year-to-year situation. Normally, I focused on the past. As I looked across the valley, I saw the evidence of deep time, hundreds of millions of years ago. After trying to understand the geology of the Uncompahgre Plateau, I was now researching the Black Canyon of the Gunnison (fig.38) and the San Juan Mountains. Plenty there to confuse me, but it was still the deep time of the past.

Could I change my focus to the deep time of the future? What would that mean? The past was visible in the rocks and mountains before my eyes. But the future? It should involve the same processes that formed the past, but it's pure speculation. Seeing the rocks of the past told us what happened to form what is there today. Speculating about the future would reverse that and go to a time and place none of us would ever see. There is no doubt that humans, as we know them, will certainly not be around 500 million years from now. Nor will the mountains and layers of rock. At least those we now see.

We can only guess what events will occur. The only certainty is what the cosmologists tell us: the sun will expand and consume the earth in about four billion years as part of its death throes. Then, oblivion. Not a pleasant thought, but we will never see it.

We can also guess that *the continents will shift, seas will expand and shrink, new mountains will rise, and existing mountains will erode to nothing. That has always happened and will continue to happen. We see such a small part of history, assuming what we see is permanent. Just as we cannot fathom the deepness of past time, we cannot fathom the time of the future.*

I am fixated on the past, although I don't regret not being there to see it. Human history has taken us from stone-age struggles to survive, to the discovery of growing our food rather than hunting it, to the explosion of technology and medicine. I wasn't here to witness or participate in that. It is as if I walked in on a movie that was halfway through. Shouldn't I be slightly irritated that I missed much of the plot? I have to settle for being satisfied that I am seeing any part of it.

But I am also aware that I won't get to see the end of the movie either. I have settled on the fact that I get to play a small part during a small segment of the movie. However, curiosity does make me wonder what happens before the eventual end.

Seeing the view in and across the valley, I have a good idea of what is next. The San Juan Mountains have eroded significantly from when they were a fiery caldron of ash and steam. The spine of the Colorado Rockies to the east was covered with glaciers not that long ago. Ice and glaciers could very well come again.

The Gunnison River has carved a narrow canyon through very hard rock. The river is at an elevation of over 5,000 feet above distant seas. The water will continue to slice through the soft sandstones and carry much of the valleys I see before me to the ocean far beyond the horizon.

But what then? Something is happening to the west in the basin-and-range-desert. Is the earth pulling apart in Nevada? How much of California will shift northward to Alaska? Will it take the Sierra with it? How does that affect our weather? It is all speculation. But it really doesn't matter.

I have to be content sitting here on a pleasant spring day, watching ravens play in the blue sky. I will patiently wait for the orchids to bloom on sunny May and June afternoons in the wet hillsides below.

They, like me, were not always here; someday the hillside will dry up and they will disappear.

We know the past. It happened and we see the result. The future is uncertain. We can only guess. The certainty of the past is comforting. It tells us why we see what we see. *The future is unknown. The unknown is always disconcerting. But it does let the imagination carry us into its beckoning arms.*

Winds and Waters of Time

I HAVE ALWAYS FOUND comfort in sitting on a lichen-covered rock, watching the full moon rise over the eastern mountains (fig.39). A light breeze on a warm night adds to the timelessness of the moment.

I could have been sitting here a million or one hundred million years ago. The moon and night sky would have been the same. The breeze would have blown gently from the west, or maybe the south, depending on how the continent had shifted on its slow journey from south of the equator.

The constellations and positions of the stars would have been different of course. The craters on the moon might have looked a little different, but the infinite blackness of the sky as it glowed with the bright reflection of the full moon would have seemed eternal. For all we know, it is eternal. At least as far as our understanding allows us to think of such a thing as eternity.

I thought of my brief journey in time. My existence compared to what I was looking at is so brief that it doesn't exist. Oh, but it does exist for me and that is all I can contemplate: existence. Each of us has an existence that is unique in the infinite history of what I see in the night sky.

When I think of what that last statement means, it humbles me but it also intrigues me. What has my existence meant? To me and to others? That is what makes each of us human.

I feel the light breeze as it gently bends the Indian ricegrass and the needle and thread grass on the hillside. I like these grasses since they belong here. They have grown on this hillside for thousands of years. As have the old, twisted junipers. A chickadee scolds me as I listen to the cawing raven soar past, heading for its night-time perch on the next ridge.

The sounds, the sights—they are the same as I would have heard and seen a thousand lifetimes ago, minus of course the buildings, roads, and fields on the mesa below me. The land—the distant mountains, the river below, the clouds fading from red to pink to purple on the western horizon—all seem timeless.

I can hear the stream below me, as the spring-fed waters start a long journey to the sea. It would be a shorter journey if they were not intercepted by the irrigators. A thousand years ago, they would have directly joined the river, then continued to the far-off sea. Not now. Too much is taken out of the river, a river that has carved canyons of color and immensity beyond our ability to understand. Once in the past, and once again in some distant future, but for now, human intervention interrupts the endless dance of air, water, and gravity. But the human actions are a small nuisance in time.

The river carving the distant canyons has had a life of its own. It sprayed energy into the air as it dove over rocks and splashed over falls. It sculpted cliffs and carried sand and pebbles to the sea, stopping occasionally to rest in calm pools. It talked to the clouds and willows along the way. The river was alive and vibrant. Now it is like a wild animal leashed and caged, passing time but no longer alive and free.

A favorite passage of mine is from Ecclesiastes. I have repeated this many times:

"Men come and go, but Earth abides."

Original peoples expressed a similar thought: only the rocks live forever.

Of course, now we know that is not quite true. In our short lifetimes, it is true; the Earth is unchanging for each of us. But over longer periods, things do change. Continents move, plants and animals become extinct, rocks erode and mountains are reduced to sand. And the universe we think is infinite and eternal is changing. Stars are born, shine brilliantly for millions or billions of years, but eventually explode and shower the universe with new elements and new life. It seems nothing is forever. All I or any of us can do is ask questions, seek answers, and marvel at the wonder of the life surrounding us.

Part IV Photo Gallery

Fig. 28: "I half thought he probably met angels...." (p. 124)

Fig. 29: "A herd of cow elk with their nursery of calves...." (p. 127)

Fig. 30: "How many birds had sat on its branches, nested in its needles?" (p. 130)

Fig. 31: "...widely spaced, squat, and many-limbed." (p. 131)

Fig. 32: "…but the flood of water drowned them." (p. 131)

Fig. 33: "Have the berries sired new seedlings, such as the younger trees nearby?" (p. 132)

Fig. 34: "...my favorite color is that edge of blue sky and white cloud...." (p. 133)

Fig. 35: "I wander down to the creek, where the tumbling water flows between black boulders and watercress." (p. 136)

Fig. 36: "You become an expert in clouds, and take that a step further and you observe the weather as it is being made." (p. 138)

Fig. 37: "Sumac was only starting to glow its yellow-orange...." (p. 140)

Fig. 38: "…now researching the Black Canyon of the Gunnison.…" (p. 142)

Fig. 39: "…watching the full moon rise over the eastern mountains." (p. 145)

Part V

Reflections on a Sense of Place

Jake's Introduction

I HAVE WRITTEN MANY things, sharing my adventures, stories, and thoughts—essentially an auto-biography—a memoir. It is now time to put in writing some of my most contemplative thoughts; these are deeper, philosophical. Having lived a long and exciting life, I want to tie it all together. Achieving wisdom has always been one of my goals. It is certainly more than accumulated facts and details (fig. 40), and I doubt if anyone knows if they attain wisdom.

As one wends his or her way through their later years, s/he thinks more frequently, "What is it all about?" We raced through youth not thinking there was an end to the future. But there is. It is like looking into the sun; I am doing that now, with increasing wind at my back. The future shortens—and the past, with all its knowledge, its critique, the confusion and mixing of successes and failures—lures us with memories. The following contemplations may only be the confused wanderings of an old man. Let us see where they lead us.

The Senses of a Place

The concept of a sense of place is not new and there has been much written about it—mostly in environmental circles as an effort to gain acceptance and understanding of environmental issues. From that standpoint, it is an effort to change behaviors between humans and their surroundings, including flora and fauna, soil and water, and promoting the idea of community.

Lately, I've found the idea taking on a life of its own; I kept coming up with new 'senses' that connect us to a place. It all depends on how you define 'sense' and 'place'. Until recently, I had simply thought about my own place, perched on the edge of a mesa, overlooking the valley and the surrounding mountains in western Colorado. Ravens Nest has provided me with numerous subjects for essays and poems over the years. This is my place and its sensory treasury has given me refuge and sanctuary in the troubled times of the early twenty-first century.

My place is a steep, rocky, jumbled patch of juniper forest, sagebrush, and streamside vegetation (cattails, watercress, sumac, rare orchids, and wild mint), at an elevation of 6300 feet. The ridge-top views encompass the North Fork Gunnison River Valley, the San Juan Mountains, West Elk Wilderness, Uncompahgre Plateau, and Grand Mesa. As a wildlife biologist, I understand the value of diversity of habitats. My forest provides escape and thermal cover, water, and a wide range of food for mammals, birds, reptiles, and insects. It also provides an escape for me from the 'outside world' which has been changing beyond recognition for this aging Baby Boomer.

The senses go beyond sight, smell, taste, hearing, and touch. They expand to whatever imagination can perceive. Place—enhanced by the senses—provides a sense of comfort, a feeling of security in a refuge. Place can be a small home, a large backyard, a small town, a community, even a region. But it combines many factors which envelop us in a warm, welcoming, comfort that we can visit and live within.

My place includes many neighbors and companions (fig. 41): juniper and pinyon, sagebrush, sego lilies, pink phlox; deer, coyotes, bobcats, mountain lions, great horned owls, ravens, chickadees, hummingbirds; biting March winds, January snows, August thunderstorms, full moons and eclipses of the sun; the rubble and basalt boulders from long ago eras, unbelievable geology of hundreds of millions of years of sandstones, shales, ancient seas and river deltas.

The senses that make up my place—so sacred to me—reflect wonder, sensuality, storytelling, relationships, movement, silence, music, diversity. As you contemplate the four essays that follow, perhaps your creative mind will lead to an appreciation of your own sense of place.

Sense of Peace

With Ravens Nest's forty acres fenced, there is a gentle feeling of enclosure. The area is defined in several ways. I can stand anywhere on the ridge tops, the slopes, or along the creeks, and feel safe. We have created a sanctuary where the rest of the world is outside. Occasionally, I have noted that the area is so peaceful that animals come here to die: a mountain lion fell over dead from natural causes; an owl hanging dead below her nest; numerous deer who never make it through winter (fig. 42). But the land is not about death. It is alive, with natural death a part of the circle of life.

We have often had guests who volunteer statements that this place feels peaceful. "There is a positive energy present here," they say. A Feng Shui master assessed Ravens Nest and said she had never felt such energy, and guided us in balancing it. Both men and women guests have felt and seen energy auras radiating around individual junipers and aura lines traversing the stream courses.

The forests, the sage flats, and stream sides are natural (fig. 43). Negative influences we see and feel 'out there' in the rest of the world, are absent from Ravens Nest. Dark forces and negative energy in parts of society today are missing here. We hike down a trail and know what the feeling was like in the Garden of Eden.

Fear does not exist. The deer is not afraid of the mountain lion, who hunts here and takes down a deer or two each winter. But it is natural. The deer runs to avoid the big cat; she is either successful or not. If she is, she does not fear the next time, it is part of her life. The rabbit does not fear the owl. The finch accepts the hunting falcon. Death is a part of life and humans fear dying, fearful of consequences that religious dogmas preach: fear of judgment after death. Life and our opportunity to live it as part of the web of interrelationships is sacred. Fear of this is a demonstration of the ignorance of our part in the drama of life.

Sense of Life

MUCH OF HUMANITY—WITH OUR amazing intelligence, curiosity, and ego—has sadly come to believe we are superior life forms. We have the power to change everything, including the inter-dependence of all living things. By doing so, we have contributed to the elimination of other life forms. This is called extinction and has been going on for millions of years. It is part of nature's way of creating new life, but not necessarily better life, at least how a human would define 'better'. Nature is amoral—there is no good or bad, better or worse.

Life surrounds us—plants, animals, insects, bacteria—life is around us all the time. We cannot escape it. We would not want to nor could we survive without it. We humans are one life form in a complex web of life; interconnections are woven like tight warp and weft.

As I walk the trails throughout Ravens Nest, I cannot help but marvel at the life surrounding me. Some life is obvious—the massive, centuries-old junipers, half dead and twisted (fig. 44), but still breathing the same air I breathe. Some life is small and seemingly insignificant—moss on boulders and meadow rue's charms. Some life blossoms into breath-taking beauty (fig. 45)—mariposa lilies and claret cups. And, consider this: most grasses produce seeds that come from inconspicuous flowers, too. But all plants reproduce like us, from pollen (male) and ovaries (female). I think humanity needs to pay more attention to how they all survive and flourish.

When I stand silent and listen, the air is full of feathered life as birds flit among tree branches and soar into the heavens. I await the arrival of hummingbirds in late April, then marvel at their acrobatics and their constant twittering. But they are not the only ones to come and go seasonally. Turkey vultures, nighthawks, lazuli buntings, black-headed grosbeaks, and many more come and go with the sunshine and frost.

I share the forest with many mammals: deer, bobcat, cougar, fox and coyote, chipmunk, ground squirrel, and even an elusive bear. They are like me—four limbs, two eyes, a nose. Come to think of it, most animals have the same form, internal and external.

I look and listen, feel and even taste, as I share their world. I am a part of it but feel left out, as I have not figured out how to communicate. I talk to the deer and watch their eyes bore into me, their ears move, their tails twitch. I know they are trying to talk to me as well, but our signals cross without understanding.

I touch the basalt boulders, alive with lichen and moss. The rock may not be living, but they are the source of the soil, necessary for life forms to live and flourish.

Pulsing and breathing, blood and sap and nutrients flow through living cells. I am part of this; we all are. We all need each other, in unknown and essential ways.

Sense of Memory

WHEN WE BELONG TO a place, we belong to a long history. We feel at one with our surroundings, which includes all living things. All living things are part of the intertwined web of life, often in ways we do not and probably cannot understand.

Just as we all have differing views of death and what comes after, we have differing views of life and where life came from. From a scientific viewpoint, life has been around for millions, even billions of years. Before that, who knows? Some have speculated that life on Earth came from out in the universe. We will leave that thought to others, but in any case, life on Earth, governed by the mysterious thing called DNA, has been bouncing around, changing, evolving, spreading its existence for time beyond our memory.

But the sense called memory may contain secrets we ignore. Or that we have not figured out how to access. A strand of DNA contains a blueprint for who each of us is, what we look like, how we behave. It also contains the history of our ancestors. We are tied to the past. We are tied to redwood trees, dinosaurs, the earliest fish in the sea, the earliest hominids—as well as our parents and great-grandparents. Whatever the first life was, it changed and evolved over billions of years into life as diverse as great blue whales, pterosaurs, buttercups, and bluebirds (fig. 46). But as far as we know, there was one beginning that started it all. And all living beings have a bit of that DNA in their cells. What a memory!

What we call memory-history is limited mostly to actions and consequences of our human relatives. When we feel the comfort and sense of belonging in a place we call home, we also feel the connection to the flora and fauna, current and past. Think about when you visited a seashore, a forest, a canyon, or a river where you felt at home (fig. 47), even if you had never been there.

Memory is our tie to the past. We think mostly of memory as our own past experiences. Memory begins at birth, although there is speculation and even claims that the growing embryo has a memory of pre-birth. We listen to the memories of our parents, older relatives, and friends, even read memories written by others. This continuous memory-history connects us to the past, weaving history into our own memory. As you may trace a thread in a tapestry, you trace a thread of the past into your own life, connecting in mysterious ways to lives unknown.

When you reflect on your sense of memory, you are connected and belong to a chain that extends into the distant past. Tapping into that memory etched in our DNA extends to the very beginning of time.

Sense of Creativity

What have I achieved? This question haunts me in my final days.

It is not necessarily a challenge to live into one's ninth decade. Good genetics and living a sensible life can achieve that. However, it is a challenge to put meaning to the past 80 years. Did I make a difference? Who did I influence and how? What is my legacy?

Rather heady questions. Some people spend their energy worrying about where they go when they leave this earth. That gets down to religious beliefs; for some, spiritual beliefs. That is the bigger picture—the metaphysical. This scares some people, maybe most people: the unknown, uncertainty.

But in all these questions, it seems my answers settle on one characteristic. It is what defines a person and how they think. It is called creativity. Creativity is the product of imagination. And imagination is the mental freedom and courage to question the deepest thoughts we can conjure up.

Imagination is not daydreaming, nor idle non-thinking. Imagination is challenging everything within you. That then leads to creativity. I have lived by a saying that I made up, but I am sure it was not original to me: if you don't question, you don't explore; if you don't explore, you don't discover; when you fail to discover, you fail to learn; when you don't learn, you don't grow; when you do not grow, you die. Questioning, exploring, discovering (fig. 48), and learning lead to creativity. How can you imagine without the stimulus of learning?

I lived in and explored the West: lakes in northern Idaho, the Cascades of Mt. Rainier, the Colorado Rockies, California's Sierra Nevada, the high plateaus of southern Utah, the Black Hills of South Dakota and Wyoming. They all are different from the cornfields of central Illinois, where I explored the little bit there was to explore. I needed more, and the remainder of my life was spent exploring all things new to me. There was a lot, and there is still a lot more, saved for the next life.

And where can we expand on our imagination and our creativity than thinking about what is next? This gets beyond the realm of our scientific knowledge and relies solely on our imagination. No one can prove you wrong. The world opens up into the universe, which then opens up into multiple universes and dimensions.

So this gets back to the question: What have I achieved?

People focus on success. In their job or career. In their collection of friends. In their accumulated status and reputation. How many people think of success as relating to their self-confidence or their ability to turn knowledge into wisdom? Success may be visible only to yourself. Which brings us back to metaphysics and beyond-the-edges-of-the-envelope type thinking. It takes courage and—guess what—imagination and creativity.

Part V Photo Gallery

Fig. 40: "...more than accumulated facts and details...." (p.157)

Fig. 41: "My place includes many neighbors and companions...." (p.158)

Fig. 42: "...numerous deer who never make it through winter." (p. 160)

Fig. 43: "The forests, the sage flats, and stream sides are natural." (p. 160)

Fig. 44: "...centuries-old junipers, half dead and twisted...." (p.161)

Fig. 45: "Some life blossoms into breath-taking beauty...." (p.161)

Fig. 46: "...life as diverse as great blue whales, pterosaurs, buttercups, and bluebirds." (p.163)

Fig. 47: "...a forest, a canyon, or a river where you felt at home...." (p.163)

Fig. 48: "Questioning, exploring, discovering…." (p.165)

Part VI

LOST IN TIME

Jake's Introduction

The Gunnison River is an ancient river, notorious for its winding path that has carved immense canyons and smaller gorges (fig. 49) through billions- and millions-of-years-old rocks. I can see the Gorge from my house. It is where the river has exited the Black Canyon but is still carving smaller canyons on its route to the sea. The water carried by the Gunnison, then by the Colorado River, originates in a distant sea, then is carried by clouds and storms that dump it as snow and rain on the jumbled and sky-high lands of Colorado. It recycles the water after a long a tortuous journey through even more immense and awe-inspiring canyon lands before it returns to another distant sea.

The ancient river and land are also ancient for humans. I recall hearing several years ago about a nearby archeological site that proved human occupation over 13,000 years ago. I didn't pay much attention, thinking it was probably well hidden in a hard-to-get-to-canyon along the river. Not long after, we had guests who learned from the local history museum about the site and how to get there. I visited the site with them; from then on I was possessed, intrigued by not just the site, but the realization that people had stood right where I was standing so many millennia ago. They were there when glaciers still draped the high country, when an ice age climate made their riverside domain a much different place than I was seeing on a cold, snowy, winter day. These were people who lived in and knew a world so different than mine, each of our worlds incomprehensible to the other.

Since that first visit, Ravens Nest (just a few miles away), became a different place to me. I now live with the spirits and energy of people I'll never know, at least in my world.

Bernice Sanderson's note:
Jake was fascinated by the Eagle Rock site, visiting many times over the years, typically during celestial milestones. In the following group of essays he explores and compares his favorite topics—geology, time and spirit—through reflection about those 13,000 year-old people.

Winter Solstice

I stopped at the edge of the cliff line as the trail wound down below me. It is steep and whoever built the trail placed large flat rocks as stepping stones to get down the small cliff. I hesitated before stepping down, and stared out at the expansive view before and below me. The clouds were low, hanging like grey sheets draping the sky, hiding the hills to the south. Light snow showers whirled white around me. The river wound through willow bottoms, hinting at its wandering and distant origin, the only sounds the soothing and timeless flow of the river.

The timeless view was only part of what I came to see. History. Not the history of the rocks and hills, which usually absorb my attention on this edge of the Colorado Plateau. Instead, I was looking for the history of early humans. The site is called Eagle Rock and I had heard the news a few years ago that evidence had been unearthed here of human habitation along the river dating back to 13,000 years—plus or minus. But I had yet to visit the site. Now was the day. The weather added to the mystery and suspense. A storm was coming in from the southwest, as many storms do. These cliffs face the southern horizon, which made me wonder at the wisdom of those people. The shelter had better be good, I thought. Otherwise, I hope they were used to wind and snow blowing in their faces. On clear winter days, however, they would feel the welcome warmth of a distant sun.

This river gorge sits on the west edge of the Colorado Rockies. From here to the rising sun, mountain ridge upon ridge extends higher and higher. Thousands of years ago, that view would have been of glacial white erupting with roiling rivers of meltwater. There would be no habitation up there. To the west, the uplands of the Uncompahgre Plateau might have held a similar ice cap or snowfields, as did the San Juan Mountains to the south. This river—gathering meltwaters from ice-capped mountains in all directions—flows north, then west again, to slickrock canyons in Utah and Arizona that were once home to ancestors of the people who lived here.

Today, my travel was only a few hundred yards downhill to the cliff-overhang dwelling place. But the significant journey for me was only in my mind as I tried to comprehend what it would have been like to live here thirteen thousand winter solstices ago. Just yesterday, the sun slowed to a stop and started its long journey back to green and summer heat, months away. The travel of the sun would have been what those people thought about. Would they have understood it wasn't the sun that moved, but the very earth that rotates in the heavens?

Did those ancients measure the sun's journey as their descendants do? There are countless sites in this desert country where rock piles and notches are prehistoric calendars. Would this site measure that? Or did these early people care beyond finding food and a better shelter from the snow and winds?

I climbed down the rock steps and hiked the trail to the lower cliffs just above the river bottom. I noticed the change from angular sandstone slabs to rounded river rocks. The river winding peacefully below me today once came up to this level and dropped the weathered and smoothed rocks it had carried for miles to this ancient shoreline. They are not sandstone, nor even basalt from the nearby volcanic mountains of Grand Mesa or the West Elks. They came from miles away, carried by the torrent of glacial meltwater that had sculpted the higher granite Rockies—maybe even the more ancient Ancestral Rockies long ago eroded to nothing.

As I rounded the last curve of the trail, winding below the insignificant-looking sandstone cliff face, I saw the wood rail fence that protects the site. Wheelbarrows and plastic buckets indicated archaeological work was still in progress, either halted for the holidays or probably the winter season. Interpretive signs, a surprise to me out here in what seemed like a distant nowhere, told the story. They said look at the cliffs for fading pictographs, or petroglyphs. They told stories from long ago, and up to recent times of Utes riding horses. The excavations dig deeply to the base of the cliff. More might be hidden under soil and rock blown in and fallen down. Had they found human remains? I had not done research before coming here, so I stood in ignorance.

I stared at the figures painted or carved on the rock. Faded, barely recognizable, but evident. Someone had stood here millennia ago writing to their gods or whomever they wanted to tell a story to. What were they saying? I had seen rock art before, but maybe not this old. Who had lived here and what was their life like? Why did they choose this overhang, which to me seemed very exposed and inconsequential?

Did they farm the river bottom (fig. 50)? One of my companions this day had read up on the history, and said archeologists had found little evidence of animal bones in the buried hearths of long ago. Were these early vegetarians? Surely they hunted meat. Was this just a quick stop on their travels or was it a permanent home?

As usually happens, I was full of questions that no one on earth can ever hope to answer with confidence. There are only guesses. This was a time so far beyond our ability to penetrate, we are strangers with no hope of finding answers.

I stood silently looking at the cliff face, then turned to face the river, not very far below. I wandered down a short section of recently constructed wooden steps built to access the water. Why were these here? Maybe the researchers needed water to wash off rocks and their digging. Or the route they brought in supplies, from the river itself. The shallow water from the ponds and sloughs of the nearby river was frozen solid. The river itself would rarely freeze, but it is several hundred yards away. What was it like thirteen millennia ago? It may have washed right up against these cliffs.

Time. The passage of time and the changes it brings have always intrigued me, especially in canyon country lined with sandstone cliffs. I let myself wander into the hanging clouds, seeing past the blowing snow, now getting heavier. I wanted to talk to these people. I tried. I closed my eyes and listened to the breeze. I heard the snowflakes hit my face, I felt the breeze carry away the sounds of the children playing here among the rocks while their parents scratched bighorn sheep figures on the rock cliff. I heard the women splashing water as they carried it in tightly woven reed baskets. An old man of thirty-five years sat hunched over fashioning a digging hoe from a piece of flint or chert.

I mentally stepped aside as a wolf-dog bounded past to chase a rabbit that disappeared into the willows. There were no sounds that would indicate what I was familiar with in my present world. The sky, hidden now by lowering clouds, would be crossed by no jet contrails, and no distant horn of passing coal trains would break the silence.

Try as I did, I could not put myself in that time in this place. It was a world that I inherited but I was a total stranger in. I felt a shiver. It was not the wind. It was a passing spirit who belonged here, coming into the future to speak to a stranger who inhabits a world he cannot fathom either. He and I lived and breathe and looked similar but can never talk with each other. People once lived here and I had come to their world, but an impenetrable barrier separates us.

Did a young boy stand here and pretend he had visited the future, seeing changes that were magic to his world? He would have looked across the river and seen a fruit orchard laid out in rows, overlooked by tall wind machines that stir the cold air on spring mornings. That would have been as foreign to him as his rock paintings are to me. Maybe the strange things he wondered about my world would have been my attempt to talk to my gods and influence my well-being. He would have marveled at the hard-soled boots that protect my feet from sharp rocks. But he would not understand the cell phone that my companion pulled out to check the weather forecast. My silent companion from long ago would not understand mountains without glaciers much less highways and automobiles with GPS mapping.

I was looking across a barrier thousands of years and worlds different from those people who lived here. I could not touch the young boy nor could he touch me. We would have seen magic and mystery in each other.

I looked one final time at the shelter site, this place of mystery slowly giving up secrets. But I knew there were some secrets it will hold forever. I started my slow climb uphill—walking through time—back to the world I feel more comfortable in. A world I inherited from men and women and children who once walked this ground but who will forever keep their world apart from mine.

This was their home; they knew nothing else, nothing more complicated than catching or growing their next meal. This is a small part of my world, the same river, the same rocks, the same grey sky. That was one answer I was looking for. Time, history, the past—it is all the same world—Earth circles the Sun, the Sun spins in its system, spinning in its galaxy, the universe of galaxies expanding and exploding in circles and cycles, never-ending, always changing.

Spring Equinox

It was the spring equinox—when the sun returns to its midway point north and now rises and sets halfway between the long glaring sunlit days of summer and the cold starlit nights of winter. I went down to the Eagle Rock site again, to see if the spiritual energy of the old people might talk to me as they did when I visited three months earlier.

What a difference. The day was sunny and warm—in the seventies— under the trademark Colorado bluebird sky. The river was running fast and muddy, early runoff awakened with a fury by unusually warm March temperatures. I could easily see the snow-capped mountains surrounding the valley. Winter had not released its grip up there, nor had a very dry spring sent the desert surroundings into a wildflower frenzy. But the feeling was anticipatory, awaiting the shift of seasons that brings so much surprise and chaos.

Some work had been done to the archeologic site, although I learned that the excavations were finished (fig. 51). Minor drainage work was being done to protect the site. I had learned much more than that— having recently attended a talk by the BLM archeologist in charge of the site. With a crowd of over one hundred, he spent nearly two hours sharing his passion for this now-famous, world-class site. He said it is one of the top sites in North America, and has surrendered the oldest basket weaving, some of the oldest petroglyphs, and a record of continuous and oldest human occupation ever found in North America.

Details, I thought, as I stood with a friend. My mind still searched for the presence of long-departed souls—souls and energy I hoped would waken and answer my questions of former lives. My friend expressed her belief that the energy of former life still hid in the willows, clung to the sandstone cliffs, wafted above the standing and running water that had come from far away snowfields.

I focused on the place, the location, the sense of home and safety that once ruled the lives sheltered here. We have coined the term *sense of place*, but what does that mean? Is there a sense of place or sacredness of home, of belonging to something more powerful than any of us?

I have been a wanderer who has only recently settled into a place I consider home. I cannot trace roots, but I do know that I come from mostly European stock. My mother's parents migrated from the hills of Tennessee to central Illinois. Where they came from before that, I have no idea, but their names suggest England, Scotland, or possibly Germany. My father's parents are also English or French English and German. At any rate, my lineage comes from vanilla-flavored European history.

This lack of a sense of ancestry and homeland has left me a searching wanderer for much of my life—for a place I feel I belong. This is something many of our ancestors experienced. Even people we think belong to a place have frequently moved. Consider the migrations from Africa to Europe, Asia, the Americas, Australia, and the Pacific Islands. When they settled a new territory, people migrated in search of the new and better, or to escape conflict. Amerindians were constantly relocating long before the newly arriving Europeans in the sixteenth century and beyond caused them to move even more.

Even with this moving, our ancestors still managed to belong to the land they lived on. They and their spiritual practices created special places, areas that had holy, sacred meanings to them. Places where they found comfort and awe. My recent ancestors did the same, not so much in locations, but in structures. Churches and temples held the sacred, honored by rituals and ceremonies; there seldom were groves of trees, rock outcrops, hilltops, or mountain lakes that held sacred meaning.

Our distant ancestors often found the energy and awe from their gods and goddesses in places that held them like a magnet. This was their sense of place—a certain location was the home of their ancestors, their spirits, their energy. If a place like this shelter called Eagle Rock had been home to a wandering people for a time that stretched beyond our comprehension, then it had to be special. It was a holy place, sacred to a people long passed to their great beyond. They are now the energy that strengthens the holiness of this location. The waves of pure energy that go unnoticed by our modern technical instruments hovered over my friend and me as we stood by the rock that had once protected this home.

I looked out over a river that has been here for untold millennia. Rounded river rock litters the ground at our feet by the shelter, but also covers the hillside far above this small cliff. This river—fed by a million years of off-again-on-again glacial highlands nearby—had thundered and rushed across this valley far above us and at our feet, maybe at a time people lived here; now below us a peaceful, muddy river that carved a deep and world-class canyon just a few miles up river.

We are surrounded by sacred. The Black Canyon upstream, the fire-born San Juan Mountains to the south, the spine of the Colorado Rockies to our east, the lava-capped Grand Mesa to the north, the uplands of the Uncompahgre Plateau to the west (hiding dinosaur remains at the Dry Mesa quarry). West of the Uncompahgre lies the vast world of Colorado Plateau slickrock canyons. Now civilization lies scattered along the edges and even within this huge sacred landscape. A sense of place, yes, but lost to most who wander throughout it today. Ten thousand years ago, did these people who once lived where I stood, understand this treasure?

They couldn't know or didn't care about the geological or paleontological significance. They probably didn't stand here and marvel at the glaciers, the future potential for tourism or mining or agriculture. They spent their efforts and attention trying to stay alive.

I cannot know what they thought about or what they felt about their surroundings. Nor will I ever be able to. Unless. Unless I could somehow talk to the spirits that float above me in the clouds forming in passing storms soon to come with lightning and thunder.

I believe they did have a sense of place, a reverence for sacredness. They didn't need a church or temple; they looked to the sky, to the river, to the cliffs. They said prayers to the antelope, the sage grouse, the sagebrush, and the running water never ceasing to flow and ripple in the river of life beyond their shelter.

Are we able to stay in one place long enough to let our own spirits gather and consecrate our forests, our cliffs, our streams? A sense of place, a sense of belonging, that is what we seek, but can we recognize it?

Humanity places the need for guidance of higher beings in the same category as food and shelter. Is this a primal human condition? Can we make decisions for ourselves? Don't we possess knowledge and wisdom to utilize our own intelligence? Must we go to a cliff and chisel pictures of spirits, construct a temple to house our protector and guide, or worship a sacred lake or seashore?

I believe I know the answer I would have gotten from the ethereal spirits of the long-ago people who sheltered here, and I have a feeling I know the answer I will get a thousand years from now. My descendants

will come to a place my contemporaries left and ask my spirit for answers.
I shout them now to the breeze coming down from the snowcapped
peaks. I tell the river—flowing out of the steep-walled canyon just
upstream—to keep my answer floating in the clouds as they build on late
spring afternoons, flashing thunder and lightning to whatever is below on
the sage-covered expanse of valley.

This is a sacred place. It has always been and will always be. It is
sacred because life existed here and still exists. Life itself is the reason for
the holy. We can label a rock, a building, a lake, with the sense of place,
but we and everything that walks, flies, swims, grows are sacred. When
we understand that, then everything will be sacred.

Summer Solstice

The new moon shared the dark sky with billions of stars, as I made my way down the trail to the Eagle Rock site on the summer solstice. Was it coincidence that this year—the year of my discovery and fascination with this archeological site—the new moon and summer solstice occurred within a day of each other? The moon and the spirits pulled me there to stand in the darkness for my quarterly visit.

The shortest night of the year drew me—to celebrate the longest sunlit day. Why wouldn't I stand there to celebrate the sun as it rose to its highest daylight point overhead? In some places, the ancients carved notches on rocks and made spiral petroglyphs to pinpoint this very day. Their ancient calendars are amazingly accurate. This is the very moment they had waited for since the low point six months earlier. The sun brought life, gave them warmth.

I felt the need to celebrate the darkness—for yin to balance yang. Some celebrate the brightness of the sunlit day. Some celebrate the darkness of the evening sky, sparkling with light that mystified the ancients: what were the lights? Were they fireflies high in the sky? Spirits of departed ancient ones? Creatures circling high in the blackness awaiting their time to descend to Earth?

None of our ancestors understood each light was a sun, possibly a sun and planet system, harboring beings like them; or a galaxy of millions upon millions of suns with countless opportunities for life. The night sky is a mystery, sacred in its hidden meanings—the total opposite of life seen during the daytime: animals and plants and mountains and rivers, all full of life, food, clothing, medicine, everything utilized by the people in their daily struggle for survival. Why not worship it?

I began to feel a lost companionship with the ancients who lived here. They watched falling stars paint streaks of light across the heavens. They watched as the flashes of lightning in summer thunderstorms lit the darkness. They saw magic in the display of power from black and roiling clouds.

No clouds this June evening as the spectacle of starlight displayed millions of twinkling stars. Shadows of darkness covered the cliffs, hiding apparitions on and across the river. Still carrying the heavy snowmelt of last winter, the flowing water echoed through the darkness.

On this night thirteen millennia in the past, a family sat by their fire, finishing their meal of roast sage grouse. Or were they lying on fur skins trying to sleep, but kept awake by the brilliance of a full moon? Maybe they were dancing to a drumbeat celebrating the longest day of the year. But did they know that? Did they chisel out a full sun or full moon on the rock panel (fig. 52)? If they did, it did not survive the countless sunny days and raindrops that slowly erase rock art.

I heard a Great horned owl in the cottonwoods across the river. Many ancient peoples worshipped the owl as the bringer of wisdom, but also as the bringer of death. The owl didn't call my name, he only called the rabbit for a midnight snack. But I am careful with these wily birds. Someday, one will call my name. Will I be ready? For the same number of millennia, they have come to this spot to call a name. Where are the graves? Where are the bones?

The night sky hides much from the knowledge and understanding brought forth in a sunlit sky. Darkness hides mysteries and awakens fears and ignorance. We celebrate the sun and cower from eclipses. We avoid dark shadows and tell stories about evils that lurk around us at midnight. An African proverb states "were the sun to rise at midnight, one would find that not only the hyena is evil."

So let us alter history and celebrate the night. Darkness allows rebirth, and the quiet to contemplate the brightness of the coming day. Darkness and light are two sides of the same coin. Rejoice in that.

Autumnal Equinox

I missed visiting Eagle Rock during the autumnal equinox. I was two weeks late, but finally stood under the October full moon, the Hunter Moon, a time when the Earth tends to ready itself for the sleep of winter. At least in the latitudes I am familiar with. Leaves had already turned color in the high country and were now turning in the lower elevations. Willows and cottonwoods were brilliant yellow; oak brush and sumac fire red and sunset orange; grasses dry, yellow-tan. All this life will provide a protective blanket to the soil, and recycle into new life soon. Summer was over and the first frost had already whitened the ground in places. Not along the river yet, but it was coming.

A full moon tends to bring out hidden mysteries, the feelings of the unknown, the strange (fig. 53). I looked at the brilliant white of the moon, now overhead, fading out the myriad of stars in the pale sky. Shadows crept over the distant mountains. Cliffs and rocks were visible in the pale darkness—alive as the brilliant orb slowly crossed the sky.

As I blinked at the brightness, I felt questions rise in my consciousness. Have I been here before? I don't mean last week or month or in recent years. Here in this exact spot, have I stood here in a past life or past time, pondering the very things I still question today?

This thought may bring up alarms if I share it with others. One doesn't bring up to strangers questions of deeply held beliefs such as religion. What is religion but the thought of something or someone higher, more powerful, more awe-inspiring than humanity? Religion is the formality of a feeling I prefer to call spirituality. I have been asking that question every time I think about the rocks forming the cliffs in this magical place. Where did we all come from? What has happened to cause all I see in the cliffs? And when and how were they formed in the long history exposed all around me?

What is this thing called life? I am the latest in our species to have roamed here, to live, and die, surrounded by and even buried in the muds and sands turned to rocks, eroded into cliffs, uncovering secrets hidden for untold millions of years. My very body is made of the same atoms that once were part of earlier beings. Do I have something called a soul? Something that goes back in time as do the rocks? Were those atoms—oxygen, nitrogen, calcium, magnesium, iron—once re-formulated as something else? Or even me or another person passing back and forth in different universes, different existences? Did I long ago stand here gazing at the full moon and shadows?

Most people have beliefs about the next world. Some don't believe there is one. Others believe in the after-life described and worshiped in various religions. I cannot speak to those beliefs since that surely is treading on sensitive ground. But it is safe to ask the questions as part of a search for truth. All of the questions and pondering I have done among these cliffs and canyons—time exposed in all its nakedness, mysteries hidden for time beyond imagination—it opens these questions for consideration.

Not only where do we come from and where did all this come from? But what is this thing called life? What spark started it all and where is it going? Where do I fit in and what comes next? Will I come back in another form somewhere in the future and stand under a Hunter Moon and look around and ask if I have been here before?

For some reason, the bright night sky seemed out of place, unnatural, although it was as natural as anything else I could see or feel. The bright white light of the full moon hides the infinite vastness of a blackness filled with galaxies and promises of other life out there. Where do I fit into all this? Such a small speck, but then the solid thing we call Earth—the home to us all, and steady and supposedly unchanging—is itself of no significance in the big picture.

I have read that the vast majority of what constitutes the universe is unknown to us. Dark matter and dark energy overwhelm the atoms of hydrogen and other elements that we can see and measure. But we have no idea what dark matter and dark energy are. Maybe they are the souls and spirits who roam on moonlit nights like this on planet Earth. And, maybe I have been here before.

Spirit Man

AFTER MY EXPERIENCE LAST month, I still can't figure out if it was a dream or real. I've slept on it, thought about it, and pondered the meaning. But I don't know for sure, although I want it to be real.

The late May afternoon was warm, with a clear blue sky, no wind, and a clean ozone smell after a rare morning thunderstorm. I can still see in my mind the amazing double rainbow that filled the eastern sky; and the accompanying quick shower was unexpected but welcome.

I was sitting on a lichen-covered boulder at the southern end of the ridge. The distant San Juan peaks were crystal clear. Most of the time when I boulder-sit, I think about the mountains, the canyon, and the rocks under my feet. That afternoon, I focused on the people who lived near here 13,000 years ago, as evidenced by the archeological site a few miles to my south. Eagle Rock had grabbed my attention. I had already written about the place and the sense of history I had when I first visited it.

Now, I wanted to see it through the eyes of the people who lived there so long ago. Who were they, what were they like, how did they live? I tried on that May day to achieve the sense of seeing the world through others' lives.

This is where I don't know if it was a dream, assuming I had fallen asleep. I think I had closed my eyes when the apparition appeared. But I felt the being. I sensed electricity in the air, the tingling on my skin. It was a man, with dark and wrinkled skin, and definite Native American features. His hair was long and pure white. He stood looking at me. He smiled.

I jumped, though that may have been imagined. I remained seated but tensed up. I blinked several times to clear my eyes since he seemed almost translucent, slightly shimmering.

I saw his lips move, but his voice seemed to come into my head more than from his mouth.

"Welcome to my world." A deep voice spoke slowly.

"Who..." I stuttered, unable to complete a sentence.

"Who am I? I live here. Or I did live here. It was a long time ago."

"How can that be? You are speaking English. How can I understand you?"

"When I lived here, English did not exist. My language was simple. We are talking, but you and I are of different times. Different worlds. In a way you may not be able to understand, I am now visiting your world.

"You want to know about my people. You are sitting on my land. This was my home. I cannot explain to you how I am here right now. You want to call it science, but I think metaphysics is more accurate. It is a mystery to me. A sacred mystery from my creator. Actually your creator as well."

He smiled again, and sat on the ground, cross-legged. Turning his head, he looked down over the valley and pointed to the river. "You call the place Eagle Rock. You have visited my home down there. But my home was all along the river for miles, not just that rock overhang. We sheltered there. By your measure, you say it was 13,000 years ago. I didn't live by counting years, or seasons. My world is gone. It was nicer than what you see now. The river was lined with tall pine and cottonwood trees. There were lots of grasses but now nothing grows. Summers were cool and winters were not so cold. This is your world now, but I was brought here by your wishes. You asked to learn about my time. This is your answer. I am here."

I just stared at him, my mouth open. Was this real? What could I say? Finally, I reached out to touch him, but I got a shock and pulled my hand back. "Are you real?"

"I could ask you the same thing. Are you real? You are a stranger to my world and I am a stranger to yours. I am as real as you are, but I think each of us is wondering the same thing. I remember coming up to this very spot one spring day. We were hunting sheep. Of course, the place looked different then. There were still glaciers covering the high mountains. There were more trees, more grass up here. The river was bigger then. It was fed by the glacial meltwater.

"You know what it looks like now? Can you wander now in what was your home?"

"I know. I wander—as you call it—in a universe different from yours. Yes, I have visited your world. I can see it but I cannot walk there with my feet in the grass. I cannot wade in the river as I did then."

"Can you take me there? Can I visit your time?" I knew what he would say but I had to ask anyway.

"You know the answer to that. When you leave your world in the future, and I think it will be soon, then you will enter mine. I am gone from the world I lived in, but I am not a prisoner of time like you are, as I was when I was alive."

"Then you are a ghost. A spirit."

"Call it what you wish. A time traveler. I can tell that is what you would give anything for. To travel in time. Be patient. You will get there. Then I can take you to see my world. But you are not ready yet."

I looked carefully at him. He was dressed in skins like he would have been in his time. "Do you have a name?"

He smiled. "Of course, I have a name. Do you? But names mean nothing. My name would be hard to pronounce in your language."

"But you are speaking my language now. Has anyone else seen you? Do you visit others in my time, or in any other time?"

He pointed south to the distant mountains. "Those peaks—I remember them as covered with snow and ice. We would travel to the base and watch the ice flow down into the valley. But I also remember when they were full of fire and melted rock."

"How can you remember that? That was millions of years ago."

He laughed. "You don't understand time, do you? Yes, it was a long time ago. But I have been there. I have also floated in the ocean that was right here where you sit right now."

"I don't understand. You lived thousands of years ago, but you were here millions of years ago?"

"What did I just say? You don't understand time. Time is a false construct. It doesn't exist. Past is present, future is past, and so on. In my dimension, we do travel back and forth. You will find out, someday." He smiled again.

"Are you God?" I asked. I didn't expect an answer.

He bent over laughing. "Am I God? Of course not. Are you God? God is another human construct. There is no one God. Each of us is our own god. We make our own decisions, create our own past and future. Do the deer grazing in the fields have a god? Does the eagle flying overhead have a god? We are all brothers and sisters of Mother Earth. Every living thing is a god and we are all connected. Who created us all? I believed in a spirit father but he wasn't a creator of the universe. He put us all here to live together. My people were part of all living things. We could talk to the eagle, the deer, the lion. You harm one, you harm us all.

"You seem to be very intelligent and full of questions. That is good. I like curiosity. That is how we learn. We taught our children by asking questions, telling stories." He looked at me, making me feel like he was looking inside me. Looking into my soul.

"Yes, I do have lots of questions, but I get this feeling you will not give me answers."

"Why should I give you answers? You know all the answers already. Just look for them."

"You are from so long ago, yet I know you are smarter than me. Were you a shaman or holy man back then?"

"Oh, here we go again. I lived long ago, in a cave, living off the land. I must be primitive, not intelligent, grunting instead of speaking. Come on, you know better than that. I was a normal person, with normal intelligence. I have the same size brain as you. Just because I could not do calculus or understand quasars or black holes, write essays on paper, or know how to light a fire with a phosphorous match doesn't mean anything.

"You could place me in the middle of what you call the Bob Marshall Wilderness, naked without anything in my hands, and I could survive quite well. Could you? Is that intelligence? What is intelligence anyway? It is understanding your surroundings and your situation in life, then come up with solutions to whatever problems you face. It is asking questions and seeking answers. Forget technology. From what I see, modern humans may have better technology and gadgets, but not the knowledge of how to use them and for what outcomes. You are way behind the curve on that one."

By this time, I was wondering if I really was talking to God. Or some form of angel. It didn't matter whether I was dreaming or facing a real spirit. Either way, I was dealing with something more powerful than me. Even if it was a dream, some power was communicating with me.

He sat there looking at the distant view. I was doing the same. High peaks in the distance in all directions. The valley below, the trees and rocks at my feet. It felt like I was on top of the world sitting at the feet of a wisdom master. Here was a chance to get answers to questions that have puzzled humans for as long as there have been humans. But I knew this being would not answer them. Or maybe could not. What more could I ask?

After what seemed like hours of sitting and talking to each other—sharing stories—he stood and raised his hands in the air. That action pulled me up to stand beside him. He began to fade, but turned and came towards me. Suddenly, a large raven appeared above his head and landed on his shoulder. He raised his hand to pet the large black head, and the bird opened his beak and squawked a loud call.

"This is Black Heart. She has been with me since I rescued her as a fledgling. It was here on this ridge. She had fallen out of her nest and her mother abandoned her. I think she had broken a toe since she limped, but it healed and she stayed with me even after I quit feeding her. She was with me for twenty years. She would leave for a few months to raise a family, then return bringing her young."

"Are you telling me that she is in the spirit world with you now?"

"Use your eyes. What do you see? Did you see a raven fly here? Do you think a wild raven would come and land on my shoulder?"

I reached out to touch Black Heart but I got a shock, like when I tried to touch the spirit man.

"I told you we are in different worlds. Different dimensions. You cannot touch me, or Black Heart."

"Why Black Heart? That seems like a negative name. To me, it connotes something sinister or evil."

"She is black, right? The heart symbolizes kindness, love, caring, life. You make what you want out of a name. You still don't know my name. It doesn't matter."

Dark clouds were forming on the southern horizon. The sun was sinking in the west. I had been here longer than I realized. Black Heart flew off, disappearing in the distance (fig. 54); my friend turned again and raised his hand.

"Can I see you again?" I asked.

"It is up to you."

"How do I contact you? And I still don't know who you are."

"You don't? Really? Think about it. Think hard. You are a very intelligent person."

I just looked at him as he grew smaller and more distant.

His voice was small and faint, but I did hear the words, "I am you."

With that, he disappeared. I didn't wake up, but it seemed I had been somewhere else. I looked around. Everything looked the same. Same rocks, same trees, same hands, and fingers. What did he mean? I am you.

Spirit Woman

I **WAS TRANSFIXED BY** the encounter with the spirit man. I never did get his name, but I will call him Black Heart, after his raven. After the vision disappeared, I stood watching the sky turn from light blue to apricot orange, then lavender. I knew I needed to get home otherwise Rachel would come looking for me. What had just happened?

It was not a dream; I knew that. I was not hallucinating; I knew that as well. I also knew I was winding down, age taking its toll. Was this a preview? Was this me? My soul?

Many years ago I wrote a story about what happens after death.[7] The character met their soul. There was no heaven or hell, not even a god. The soul was the person, or more correctly, the person was the personification of the soul. Was that what I just encountered? My soul came to visit since I had called out to him? I was not ready to join my soul yet, but was the soul telling me the time was close? And would I then get to accompany them on a trip to visit my past or my soul's past?

I didn't tell Rachel, but she seemed different. When she looked at me, I felt she was looking at a stranger. I did not sleep well that night. I kept reliving that afternoon. Who was this person? He said he was me. Or I was him. Was I a reincarnation of him? Of me? But he said he had been here millions of years ago. If he was my soul, were there souls before there were people? And this thing of communicating with each other—how did we do that? Maybe it was a dream.

Did I have a connection with his world? Was I really here 13,000 years ago? Surely I would have had many other lives since then. Why hadn't I been visited by some other person? A Viking visiting the shores of North America. An Inca shaman. A Chinese Zen master. A Polynesian sailing to discover Hawaii. What have I had an interest in over my lifetime? Was I Thomas Jefferson or Teddy Roosevelt?

I finally fell asleep but did not dream. Or was I still in a dream?

The next day was cloudy, with an approaching storm carrying the remnants of tropical storm Rudolfo tracking up the California coast from Baja. I felt someone or something calling me. It called me to the

---

7   Alistair Corey included this in the "Tales of Ravens Nest" collection he edited soon after Jake and Rachel passed.

bridle.[8] I put on my raincoat, expecting rain any minute, and walked out to Ravens Nest's north gate, near where the bridle was still hanging in the juniper. Discovered by Rachel only recently after hanging there for decades unseen, I wrote a story, finding the tale easy to construct—although I didn't know where it came from in my head.

Now, as I approached the juniper, a few raindrops fell. The bridle was there, but I had to rub my eyes since it seemed to glow. My eyesight is greatly improved since cataract surgery, but I had trouble focusing on the leather reins. I felt a tingling, especially in my hands, as if coming out of numbness. I heard a horse whinny, although I wasn't aware of our neighbor's horses being anywhere nearby. Then I saw the vision: a young woman on a brown and white paint horse. She had ridden down from the north and was laughing.

I dropped the stick I had picked up at the base of the tree and stared at her. She pointed to the tree and said, "There it is! My bridle. I knew it was up here. It looks good (fig. 55)!"

For the second time in two days, I was dumbfounded. She reached out for it, but her hand went right through it. "Right," she giggled. "I cannot touch it. Or you."

Finally, I stuttered, "Your bridle?"

"Yes, I made it. You made it."

"Oh no," I moaned. "Not again. I am you. You are me?"

"I suppose you don't remember, do you?"

"What is happening to me? It was a man 13,000 years old and now it is the person who made this bridle 200 years ago? And you both say, 'I am you.' What is magic about this place?"

"Oh, it is not magic. I have never been here before. But I knew I had to come. You called me.

"I didn't call you."

"Maybe not your conscious thought. Or maybe not the Earthly-you but the spirit-you. Your soul."

The rain was coming down a little harder, but I noticed her long black hair was not wet. The horse was not wet.

"You are not wet," I said as I looked at her.

---

8   And Alistair included this in "The Hermit of Puccini Ridge," the second collection he edited.

"Is it raining? Oh, it doesn't matter. I am not there with you. Don't ask me to explain. I don't understand it."

I noticed the bridle was on the horse. It was also on the tree.

"You reunited with your horse. Was the story I made up true? You made the bridle, came over the mountain with your horse, then lost the horse and lost your land. Is all that true?"

"You should know. Yes. Thunder was my brother's horse. I saved him but not my brother or family. I lived down below for many years. My sons were born there and were forced to leave with me to the Reservation. I loved it here. I may not have set foot on this place, but we would spend summers up on Thunder Mountain. Just up there." She pointed to the top of Grand Mesa.

"Then the whites came and caused me great pain once again. I lost Thunder and the bridle I made for him. You are white but we have been many things over the years—you are multi-cultural."

"I would like to meet them all, but not the way this is happening." I groaned as I leaned against the tree.

"Oh, you will. I have. It is fascinating. I guess you can say I am multi-cultural, too."

The rain was letting up to a light drizzle, but she and the horse remained dry.

I heard what I knew was a wolf howl. I looked at her, ready to ask the question, but I hesitated.

"What did they call you? What is your name?"

"I don't know your name either, but it doesn't matter. I was called Golden Swan. I won't try to tell you my Indian name. Too many vowels." She chuckled when she said that. "And by the way, I know you heard him. Midnight is coming up behind me. Yes, Midnight is a wolf. He is my friend. I rescued him when he was a small pup. His mother and den mates were killed and I found him alone and scared. He would have starved to death. He was with me for years. Of course, now he is with me forever. As is Thunder."

"Midnight seems a strange name. I wouldn't think you had a word for that time of night."

"Oh, of course, we didn't. It is my translation. Midnight is an invention; it is clock time and we didn't have clocks. The real meaning is something like *dark of night*." Though apparently younger than Black

Heart, Golden Swan was also wise and knowledgeable, multi-cultural, and with a sense of humor. I was expanding my acceptance of what seemed totally unbelievable. But I was seeing and hearing too much to not believe.

I was being pulled into something I didn't understand, but my curiosity had pulled me to many places in my life. Or was it in my lives? I shouldn't be surprised, I thought. I had written about this life after life. Parallel universes with multiple lives with one soul or spirit. No heaven or hell or god or judgment. Just life after life. Well, I was being shown this now. Again.

In for an ounce, in for a pound, I thought, so asked, "What can you tell me about your experiences?"

"I can see you are very confused. Don't worry. That is normal. You should have seen me when I discovered this reincarnation thing."

"But you seem so, what? How can I describe it? You are very intelligent and way beyond the awareness that you lived in."

"You mean how can a barbarian girl who couldn't read or write or tell time or know anything about history or philosophy be so advanced?"

"I don't mean to be condescending, but I guess that is what I am saying."

"Talk to any of your past selves. You will find us all very up-to-date on everything that has ever happened."

"We are timeless. Is that what you mean?"

"Think about it. You and I and dozens of others are a representation of our soul. A powerful intellect that sends each of us in our time to Earth to live. The soul learns from the many experiences it has already encountered. Some are new. They are cumulative. I don't know where this force comes from. I don't know what it will do with all this knowledge. Maybe it passes on, to become a god in another universe. I don't know what happens to each of us. When I died, I got to visit with this being. I was able to visit others who were my counterparts. Then I disappeared. I am not living some continuation of my life nor am I living in a heaven or nirvana."

"Was this rather unnerving to you?"

"As you know, I was an Arapaho girl born on the other side of the mountains about 100 years before you. I suffered the loss of my family to barbarian white people. I met a young warrior, moved over to this side of the mountains, raised a family, and had my land taken away by more barbarian white people. I was moved to an unfamiliar land and forced to live there, where there was no food nor a way to live the life I was born to live. Then I died a lonely old woman and discover all the things we are talking about. Unnerving? Well, I guess it was difficult to absorb. So now I tell you to expect the same thing because you and I are the same person. But your experiences are totally different than mine. And you will soon get to share all the lives of your doppelgangers."

"Okay, it is weird beyond belief. Do you know if everyone is the same as us? Does everyone have a soul and multiple brothers and sisters in different lives?" I was still mesmerized. I could spend all day talking with her.

"You are a deep thinker. You will find all this out and I am told fairly soon. But no, talking to me is not the same as talking to your, our—soul. I am well informed and can tell you that we are part of a select group. Many beings are just people—humans, mammals, part of the web of life on this planet, walking and talking, that you and I met every day of our lives. They are the people who don't seem to think deeply and broadly. They don't get the big picture, they are just getting by. Think of the intellectual, creative, curious people."

"Okay. I get the picture. I think of the boring people, the cruel people, the people who…" I faded off. No need to keep going. Now, a lot made sense to me.

The rain had stopped and the sun was falling behind clouds in the western sky. I wanted to hug Golden Swan, to pet Thunder, to touch Midnight. But they were starting to fade. Golden Swan held her hand to me as she backed away. "It has been a pleasure and we will meet again. Farewell for now." She turned and Thunder trotted away, with Midnight loping behind. The wolf turned and stopped. He looked at me, then lifted his head and howled. A howl that went through my heart.

I touched the bridle. It felt warm. I stared at the adjacent field, where I last saw them. It was empty. I closed my eyes, trying to get one last glimpse, trying to hear another howl.

A lot to think about—I guess first on my mind was that both visitors had commented that my time was almost up. Could be. I am getting up there in years and I have been slowing down. My lungs are compromised and I can't climb up ridges like I used to. I've led a full life with no regrets.

I walked to a nearby boulder and slowly sat down. I didn't know anyone I could talk to about these experiences. Not even Rachel. Did I talk to God? I guess that depended on one's definition of God. I don't believe in the vengeful, judgmental God of the Old Testament who created everything and judged everyone. I believe that humans created god, not the other way around. Think about how many gods there are: pagan goddesses, Man Above, Great Spirit, Yahweh, Allah, the Hindu gods, and all the rest. But my soul? Is it really a god? No, it is an advanced intelligence that is pure energy. Maybe that is the god people want to exist. This whole religion subject is touchy. There are some people I can't discuss it with. There are lots of disagreements and strong feelings. Is one right and all the others wrong?

But my personal god doesn't judge me. It is me. Or I am it. I don't understand how that works. And Golden Swan said not everyone has a soul. Are we special extra-terrestrials? I've pondered deep questions like this most of my life; maybe it's time to find out. What is next? Maybe nothing. Maybe a whole new world. I think it is time.[9]

---

9   Judging by his date notation, this was the last thing ever written by Jake. He and Rachel left this Earth three days later. They were together and as far as we can tell, decided to leave and they did it by thought alone.

Part VI Photo Gallery

Fig. 49: "...notorious for its winding path that has carved immense canyons and smaller gorges..." (p. 175)

Fig. 50: "Why did they choose this overhang...? Did they farm the river bottom?" (p. 177)

Fig. 51: "… I learned that the excavations were finished." (p. 180)

Fig. 52: "Did they chisel out a full sun or full moon on the rock panel?" (p. 185)

Fig. 53: "A full moon tends to bring out hidden mysteries, the feelings of the unknown...." (p.186)

Fig. 54: "Black Heart flew off, disappearing in the distance...." (p.192)

Fig. 55: "There it is! My bridle. I knew it was up here. It looks good!" (p. 195)

Part VII

Bernice Sanderson's Epilogue

CENTER OF THE UNIVERSE

WITH THIS, I CLOSE the final book of Ravens Nest. I say goodbye
to Jake and Rachel, Al and Tori; may their souls rest in the peace and
beauty they found here. I also close a significant portion of my life. My
young life was what I would call normal in childhood and through college. Even though I did not grow up on a farm, I always liked the rural,
agricultural lifestyle. When I applied for and received the internship
at Ravens Nest, I didn't dream it would become my life. I came here to
learn about sustainable agriculture and nutrition, and loved working
the soil. I guess I showed something Tori liked. She hired me and things
kept growing and changing. I fell in love with Ravens Nest and all the
people here. And here I am half a century later.

I never knew Jake and Rachel. Because Tori was so close to Jake, she
shared her knowledge of him with me. Through my reading and closing

out the second edition of "Tales of Ravens Nest," I gained much insight. Ravens Nest affected many people. I cannot say this was all due to Jake, but he started a cascade of events that changed this area, and Tori was instrumental in all these changes. Her music alone changed many people.

With my discovery of the final batch of Jake's writings, I had to deal with all the new revelations by myself. Tori had passed, and so too my beloved Robbie—the guiding light for much of my life. As I read Jake's final thoughts, I found myself traveling his journey. At times, I wished I could talk with him, but realized I was; I couldn't hear his answers, but by this time, I had a really good idea what those answers would be.

I was never a religious person and I know Jake nor Tori were not. But they were very spiritual and always were looking very broadly and openly, understanding the sacred. I was also influenced by Robbie and her beliefs. As I read Jake's manuscripts, at times I felt that I was witnessing another universe, peeking into the cosmos and seeing what is really out there. Or in here, in our hearts and souls. We, as a component of this thing called life, have strayed afar, looking to other or others to direct our lives. We have delegated too many of our decisions and beliefs to gods, saints, or political leaders. That is a dereliction of personal responsibility.

Jake's 'final' essay was a blank sheet of paper with the title *Center of the Universe*. No one will ever know what he was going to say. It is eerie that Tori wrote and recorded a song of the same name. Maybe Jake discussed this with her or maybe they were so in tune with each other, she captured his thoughts. Jake was fascinated with the universe, time, eternity, the interrelationship of all life. We are all connected and are all part of a cosmic energy we call life. As an old saying goes, "It is up to us," both individually and collectively. I close this volume with my own thoughts on this subject.

After the earthquake devastated the original Ravens Nest house and I found Jake's hidden writings, a fierce storm pounded the area with three inches of rain, followed by 50-mile-an-hour winds. Quite a few trees were toppled, including several of the many large and centuries-old junipers on Ravens Nest. One in particular was significant—next to where the original Opal cabin stood. Still alive when Jake and Rachel came here, it became a snag in the years after Alistair died. It uprooted with a large root ball: the soil, rocks and boulders embedded within the massive roots rises nearly four feet above the ground.

Studying the root ball and the hole it created, I noticed something gleaming in the sunlight. Carefully scraping away mud, I exposed a gallon-size canning jar with the lid still on tight. I gasped when I saw what was inside: it was filled with coins. There had been some leakage over time and both outside and inside were stained with the lime coating found under most rocks here at Ravens Nest. I looked around to see if anyone was watching me, but the place seemed deserted on that momentous afternoon.

Afraid I would break the glass by moving it—coins are heavy!—I pondered how to approach its extraction. I filled a bucket with water, fetched a blanket and rags, a large wrench and some lubricating oil. After gently removing mud and rocks to expose the jar, I spread the blanket next to the hole, and—with baited breath—rolled the jar onto the blanket. The lid was tight, but judicious use of the wrench and oil finally loosened it. I poured the contents onto the blanket and methodically wiped the coins with wet rags, then piled them in stacks.

Most were gold, some dated in the late 1800s. A few old silver dollars were mixed in. There were $20 double eagles, four $10 gold Indians, and several $5 gold half eagles. I realized the value was not the silver and gold, but the numismatic or coin value. This had to be the jar that Opal buried long ago, then lost the map where she buried it, and totally forgot about it. Tori had mentioned that Jake always thought someday he would find a jar of buried money. Well, here it was. From what I knew about Opal, I could not understand how she had this treasure. Or was it something Willy found or stole? But then, maybe it wasn't such a treasure over 100 years ago, and Opal would not have appreciated the value. Regardless, I knew this discovery closed the circle and was the end of a long and intriguing story.

What to do? I made an appointment with the nearest coin dealer, who was speechless when I spread the coins across his shop counter. Tallying up the value, he gave me a note with the figure $32,000 written on it, and I almost fainted.

I knew this treasure legally belonged to the Institute, but how to deal with it? I struggled with the dilemma for a week, and took out a small handful of coins. I then gave the jar to the council, who decided to donate it and the contents to their museum. With some of the coins I kept, I bought two simple ground-level headstones for Opal's and Willy's graves in the local cemetery.

After the destroyed house was removed and the site cleaned up, my remaining coins were enough to buy two small engraved marble monuments—one dedicated to Jake and Rachel and one for Al and Tori—and had them placed on a concrete pad where the original house stood. The Institute embraced my suggestion that these become the center of a basic seven-circuit labyrinth. This would become a sacred place for visitors of all faiths, especially to the tribal elders who remembered Jake and Tori with deep fondness.

The night before I moved away, I walked the labyrinth and kept private vigil at the monument. I lit a candle and lay down on the ground. Knowing Jake had been entranced by the cosmos and deep philosophical issues about time and eternity, I looked up at the sky and thought about the universe, the stars, galaxies, and deep time. I knew Jake, Rachel, Tori, Al—and my Robbie—were out there somewhere in some form. I didn't know much about cosmology or the universe, but I was mesmerized by the twinkling dots filling the sky. We are passing specks in a vast universe that involves such an eternity of time, it was hard to focus. I knew Jake would have understood.

I also thought about Tori and her music. *Labyrinth* is a song of hope, yet sad and mournful. One of my favorites is the instrumental *Cosmos*. In it, she plays her cello, organ and harp. I was with her when she recorded it and cried as I heard her play. Another favorite she recorded in Jake's memory. I knew she loved Jake as a father; he was the inspiration for many of her songs. *Center of the Universe* is an instrumental, although she did compose lyrics for it, which are printed in the album insert. The words tell how each of us is the center of a universe that expands to infinity in all directions. We can sit on Earth and watch shooting stars falling to Earth, but our souls and conscious thoughts fly out in all directions toward the stars and galaxies. Although scientists and astrophysicists say there is no point where the Big Bang occurred and thus there is no center, in effect, each of us is the center of the cosmos and travels as photons of light forever.

Laying there within the labyrinth, I played Tori's songs on a portable player. As I watched the night sky, with my photons flying, the

candle flickering in the light breeze—throwing dancing shadows on the monuments—I knew I had been living in, but now would be leaving, a sacred place. I also knew I needed to leave. There were too many sad memories for me. This was a final goodbye and the end of a long story of people I loved. As Opal once read, "Men come and go, but Earth Abides." Everyone I had known at Ravens Nest was gone or soon would be. We had come and gone. Ravens Nest was still here and would be for as long as the universe looks down on this sacred place—the center of the universe.

Author Acknowledgments

When I began writing the short story "Tori's Dream," I never imagined where it would lead. It opened up another world. It led to Al and Tori, Jake and Rachel, Bernice, and back to many memories accumulated during my life. So, I must thank these fictional characters, whom I have grown to treat as my family. They inhabit my books *Tales of Ravens Nest*, *Hermit of Puccini Ridge*, and now, ending in *Flight of the Raven*.

In all my books, I am grateful to a world-class designer and book expert, Connie King of Constance King Design. She has produced wonderful book covers as well as content design.

And of course, someone who deserves to be listed as co-author, but settles only as editor: Katherine, who has shepherded all my books through the long processes, while still creating her world-class artwork.

About the Author

ALTHOUGH HE GREW UP in a small Illinois town, Joseph has spent over 50 years living and working across the West. During his college years at the University of Idaho studying forestry and wildlife management, he worked in Idaho State Parks, and Mt. Rainier and Grand Canyon National Parks. He then spent over 27 years with the US Forest Service in five different national forests in four states. After retirement from the Forest Service, he spent ten summers doing fire information work on wildland fires, assisting the media and homeowners in understanding wildfires. As a second career, Joseph Colwell has authored seven books.

Joseph and his artist wife (and editor) Katherine now own and live on their 40-acre nature preserve in western Colorado. They specialize in assisting others in exploring creativity, using nature as the source of inspiration. They can be reached through ColwellCedars.com or jcedarsj@gmail.com.